Dubliner **Ian Macpherson** is a writer and performer. His work includes one-man shows, scripts for various media and this, his first novel. He passes his days writing, reminiscing, and polishing his many awards.

Deep Probings

Deep Probings

The Autobiography of a Genius

IAN MACPHERSON

© Ian Macpherson 1999

First published 1999
Thirsty Books
an imprint of
Argyll Publishing
Glendaruel
Argyll PA22 3AE
Scotland

The author has asserted his moral rights.

All events and characters in this book are
entirely fictional.

**British Library Cataloguing-in-
Publication Data.
A catalogue record for this book is
available from the British Library.**

ISBN 1 902831 09 8

Cover art
Tracey Holland

Origination
Cordfall Ltd, Glasgow

Printing
ColourBooks Ltd, Dublin

For Tom, Fergie and Declan.
They'll know why.

Ah woe!
Ah woe! Alas! Pain, pain ever, for ever!

1

It is not for me to draw parallels between my own life and that of Christ. But ponder this: I entered public life in millennial times; I wrote my masterpiece in a two hour burst after a twenty nine year gestation period; and true, Christ was crucified while I was merely held on remand, but I'm willing to bet he experienced similar difficulties getting the Bible published. This is the trouble with genius. When the film rights are eventually sold it can often be up to two thousand years too late for the author to cash in.

But I wonder if Christ suffered, as I did, in his formative years. I imagine him sullenly holding a handful of nails while his earthly father put the finishing touches to a kitchen cupboard, reflecting, not without justification, that his mind was on higher things. Whereas, at a certain age we MacFiachs were expected to become tillers of soil and hewers of wood before school, after school and, later on, where school used to be. Now the artist, not unlike the saviour, must have time to inhabit an elevated plane of consciousness; to dwell on matters sublime. My father either didn't understand this or chose to ignore it and we were encouraged to dirty our hands at an early age in the ultimately futile battle against nature. Digging. Milking. More digging.

My father would begin with broad hints about the field above or the lambing season being particularly busy. If that didn't work, your wellington boots would be placed beside all the other wellington boots in time for the next dawn exodus. If you chose to ignore this hint the boots would stand as a constant reminder throughout the day. They would be admired by all for their cleanliness and paraded in front of visitors in a heavily ironical way.

With my brothers this form of primitive psychological warfare worked on the first day, but I was made of sterner stuff. It may not have been obvious to my parents – being simple peasant folk – that I was touched by genius, but the following scene must have given them some sort of clue.

I had spent several days ignoring the boots, the hints, the nudges, the winks, and happily exerted myself instead on my noble calling. On one such occasion my mother was bent over the kitchen sink scouring her interminable pots when my father returned from work followed, in descending order of seniority by Ferdia, Fintan, Fergal, Feardorcha, Fachtna, Fiachna, Francis, Fergus, Finian, Fadharta, Fursa, F. X., Flann, Finn and Fats. I had sixteen brothers but nothing, as I recall, in the way of a sister. All were about to remove their soil-encrusted boots after a hard day in the fields and place them beside my immaculate pair as a prelude to their muscle-bound banter when they spied me spread out on the floor with pencil and paper. Silence fell, broken only by the scouring, the squelch of boots, the pipe suck. The drumming of my fingers on the page. I, Fiachra MacFiach, was about to produce my first word. They stood round in a circle and I could feel them thinking, yes, he *is* different.

They were transfixed, rooted to the spot, mesmerised by the poetry of this unforgettable scene. I could describe the tension of the moment; how the neighbours drifted in and cheered me on; how my father lost a modest sum when the word wasn't 'Father'. But this is not a cheap and sentimental novel. I don't propose to milk the tension for dramatic effect. I was the centre of attention. I was intellectually advanced beyond my years. Enough. I merely record that I took that first historic leap onto the page with a bold if illegible squiggle. The word I was struggling towards was 'Spawn'. The main topic of conversation afterwards: why I had chosen to write it with my foot. But who knows, for who can comprehend the mind of genius?

This turn of events confused my father for a while. The boots stayed where they were but he seemed less sure of his ground. Perhaps I *was* different, he seemed to be thinking. That evening, at any rate, he whipped out his melodeon and began playing a jig, perhaps in celebration of my emerging otherness. It was, I suppose, a small price to pay.

If my own ingenuity kept my boots clean up to a point, it was luck which played a bigger part in allowing me to develop at my own pace. I have mentioned several of my brothers, omitting only the last born. In much the same way that nowadays every Irish household produces a well-known novelist, in those days the youngest child was destined for the priesthood. So it was with little 'Father', and from an early age he was afforded the preferential treatment of the chosen one. That this state of affairs was monstrously unfair is beyond question and illustrates the unequal standing of art and religion in the Ireland of those dark times. I, the artist, was expected to soil my hands like a common labourer while Father was treated with fawning servility at all times.

I suffered his outrageous assumption of superiority with saint-like stoicism for the most part, helped no doubt by not having a jaundiced bone in my body. Had I been the jealous type I might have been infuriated by his self-satisfied expression, the work-shy softness of his hands, the deference accorded him as a child of the cloth while I, his superior in all matters, was treated like the common herd. Yes! If I had been in any way capable of envy, I say, my poetic soul would have blackened with rage and I would probably have pummelled the doe-eyed little scut to an early grave. As it was I bore this monstrous, this shameful, this crying-out-to-heaven injustice with remarkable and commendable fortitude. True, I was accused on more than one occasion of violence but this was mostly the result of youthful high spirits and usually consisted of nothing more than sitting on his head or, on one memorable occasion, trying to give him a bath in the kettle.

I was severely punished for the latter, forced to confess to the little blighter and given three Hail Marys, an Our Father and, worse, full absolution in a 'magnan-

deep probings

imous' gesture of reconciliation. I resolved that the next time I gave him the kettle bath treatment I'd put his head in first.

The fact that he was destined for the priesthood meant that his nappies, his romper suits and his first surplice were all of finest clerical black. He finally graduated to full evening dress with tri-cornered hat at the age of two and would glide around the house tut tutting at my artistic endeavours or blessing my mother as he passed the sink. And I have to admit it, in the eternal struggle between art and religion he seemed to have secured an easy victory for the men in black. He would have suited the job well. He had the soft hands from an early age. He only had to work on the sanctimonious look. That he never got the chance to develop beyond the hands owes much to the MacFiach dynasty's eating habits.

Because of the number of children involved, a large tureen of our staple diet, the ubiquitous Kerr's Pink potato, was placed at the head of the table and the contents passed along. It was the responsibility of each child to look after the next in line. Ferdia to Fintan to Fergal to Feidhlim and so on. The pot having been placed on the table, potatoes were fired expertly from hand to smaller hand. Is it any wonder that eight of my brothers played the execrable game of rugby for Ireland, their proudest moment being 'the glorious missed try of '73'? The ball, as they are apt to recount, passed between all eight of them. It was subsequently tossed, just under the post, to the present writer, who wasn't, I am more than happy to report, there.

So it was with the potatoes. Down the line they came,

each child feeding his younger sibling with a skilful sideways pass. Until, that is, they came to me. I must, at this point, broach the delicate subject of my shortcomings: the need to fulfil my exalted destiny, to exclude trivia. This is not, strictly speaking, a flaw – it is, in certain respects, an admirable trait – but it can lead to unfortunate consequences. And so it proved on this occasion.

I recall remarking to one of my brothers that I hadn't seen little Father for some time.

'Father,' he said pointedly, 'is dead.' And, although I hadn't actually asked, 'Malnutrition,' he added, equally pointedly. This would perhaps explain why my mother was attacking her household chores with less than her usual brio. And why dinner was infuriatingly late for some time to come.

It might be felt by some of my more impressionable acolytes that Father's end was in some way hastened by a misguided attack of sibling rivalry on my part. Nothing could be further from the truth. My poet's soul was otherwise engaged; I had simply failed to notice the little feller.

A verse I wrote some time later captures the poignant mood:

> It's hours past dawn
> But the curtains are drawn
> You're still in your bed
> They tell me you're dead
> You were so I'm told
> Just three short years old
> But God! I got riled
> When you called me 'my child'.
> *(from the Irish)*

This sequence of events could hardly be seen as auspicious.

deep probings

Happily, however, I was vindicated by the parish priest – also called Father – who insisted that it was God's will. He went further. He came over to where I was sitting and patted me on the head.

'What God is telling us,' he purred, 'is that this child here is destined to be the priest.'

I was too young at the time to understand the implications of this outrageous synthesis or I would have debated the matter there and then. As it was the debate came later. In the meantime, I enjoyed all the privileges of the priest to be. My boots were removed from the line. I was treated with due deference. My parents called me 'Father'. I was given a large tub of moisturizing cream for my hands. I was a poet with the perquisites of a priest but none, as yet, of the responsibilities. That day would come, of course, but in the meantime I set about taking advantage of my new-found status.

I could describe in minute detail the months that I lorded it over the household as 'Father'. I was granted, for a while, the luxury of doing as I pleased, but the artist was born to suffer and I thank the parish priest for giving me the opportunity to return to a life of misery.

One day, when I had developed the smug expression, unctuous manner, sanctimonious turn of phrase and delicate hands of the cleric in embryo, I was summoned to see him. My career had been mapped out, he enunciated. I would serve him as an altar boy, moving on to the position of head altar boy and from there leaping forward from novice to curate to priest, parish priest, bishop, archbishop, cardinal and, 'the Lord save us, perhaps the Pope himself!'

'Pope Fiachra the First,' he chortled, rubbing his flaccid hands together with relish. 'Let's make it happen.'

I studied him carefully to see if he was perhaps jesting. He wasn't. It was, granted, an interesting career plan, but the artist can have no truck with corporate structures. I pointed this out to him in the vocabulary I had available to me at the time.

'Nonsense, my child,' he said, and had the temerity to suggest that the ability to rhyme was a passing phase and that I'd grow out of it as I matured.

'On the contrary, my child,' I replied. I spoke to him of the preoccupations of the poet: frog spawn, galoshes, the difficulty of writing in a language where nothing rhymes with orange.

As I developed my theme he sat meekly phrasing his reply, his soft, plump hands intertwined in an attitude of humility, his lips moving in sibilant near-silence as he worked on his forthcoming speech.

'A nice point, my child,' he began, 'but consider this. God has called you. End of story.'

'Perhaps I could have that in writing, my child,' I replied, not untetchily.

'And what leads you to suppose that God, the God of wrath and hell-fire, the all-knowing God, the God of rage, of ire, the great God almighty, has time for personal correspondence, my child?' said Father.

I must say that I was beginning to find his debating tactics negative in the extreme. God had called me. He didn't wish to discuss the matter. Father was pursuing a narrowly Jesuitical line of argument. I, ergo, would have to borrow from a different spiritual model. So deciding, I

deep probings

gave him the full force of my left galosh on his shin in the fond expectation that he would go away enlightened.

He might indeed have done so in a different setting but I had ignored the pertinent fact that it was his home. He contented himself with hobbling after me as *I* went away.

'Priest killer,' he cried. 'I know where you live.'

If the latter was meant as a threat it wasn't needed. By the time I arrived home my parents had got the message: I was no longer to be the priest. All bets were off. My father started dropping hints. Heavy hints, sometimes with an undercurrent of menace. He also knew where I lived.

2

The showdown, when it came, left me with no option but to accede to my father's heinous demands. I was inserting an early attempt at aphoristic wit into my journal when I noticed him standing over me.

'The field above,' he said, 'is ready for the plough.'

I glowered at him.

'There's still some daylight left.'

In the parlance of popular culture this was a bad Western. I stared him out.

'I believe there's a spade in the cow shed,' he snarled.

I raised my pen majestically.

'This, Sir, is my spade! I'll dig with it.'

Foolish words. Metaphorical language is sadly wasted when discussing manual labour with the peasant class. He yanked me up to the field by the collar of my jacket and I ran through a full set of nibs before his mood softened back to dour.

deep probings

'Have it your way,' I fumed. 'Where's the cow shed?'

It goes without saying that the true artist must have time to chew the cud of his thoughts. To this end he should drink only sufficient alcohol to merit the prefix 'tortured'. He should lie low during the breeding season. Above all, he should avoid manual labour. And yet. And yet. A spot of honest toil is not without its compensations. I began to place selected poems by my fellow versifiers in the cracks of dry stone walls and work towards them. I later realised that it was quicker to walk straight over to them and the spade became merely a handy instrument to lean on as I read. In this way the walls soon became littered with verse. Lo a Yeats. Yon a Joseph 'Mary' Plunkett – a fine poet and openly transsexual before there was money in it, and at a time, indeed, when a job in the civil service might depend on withholding such facts.

My father used to watch me often from the house as I leaned over the spade reading. Paternal pride? I like to think so. He effected to think of me as a waster and a fool and yet secretly he was very proud of me. Many years later I was incarcerated at Her Majesty's pleasure and my father's wallet was found to contain, on his death bed, a faded transcript of the court case.

This exalted state of leaning on my spade reading might have continued indefinitely had I not been jolted out of it by the machinations of one of my less fortunate brothers. When I refer to Fadharta the Simple as less fortunate I am merely referring to the yawning gap in our respective intellects. On a scale of nought to ten we are separated by the latter, but although Fadharta was simple he was sly with it.

I was first alerted to his devious nature by an incident which shocked me to the marrow. It is well known that Irish fields are filled with stones. Always. This is referred to as the second sorrowful mystery of agriculture. The first sorrowful mystery deals with the fact that the Irish small farmer is always in possession of a three-day growth. Never two. Never four. Three. This has never been adequately explained, but I have solved, inadvertently, the mystery of the stones.

I was leaning on my shovel reading, as I recall, a witty dissection of machismo in the civil service by Joseph 'Mary' Plunkett when out of the left curve of my eyes I spotted Fadharta removing stones from his field *by putting them in mine*. So stunned was I by this flagrant breach of the unwritten code of the countryside that I almost fell off my spade. Here was my giant, foolish brother taking advantage of my genial nature – another character weakness, I'm afraid – to present his own field in a more favourable light. I was apoplectic. Granted the farm had its fill of walls and each wall had its fill of stones. Some of the walls in the more exposed corners of the farm were even protected from the buffetings of nature by other walls. There was, I admit, nowhere else for a stone to go. But Fadharta's solution to the age old question, albeit the brainchild of a simpleton, was provocative in the extreme.

He was dealing with a mind, however, at the sharp end of the spectrum. I waited for him to go. I moved his stones back. I added a few stones of my own to let him know I meant business. There the matter rested until the following morning. I went and stood in my own field as was my wont and cast wry sidelong glances at Fadharta over The Boys' Own Book of Polish Verse. He was scratching his head in puzzlement, accentuating his moist and protruding lower lip which flapped disconcertingly when he attempted speech. That he attempted it at this time illustrates the level of his confusion, but his deviousness finally won out over his simplicity and by midday the stones were back in my field.

This state of siege and counter siege continued for three months. Fadharta took to moving the stones back last thing at night which caused me to undo his work before cock crow. Not that I should have bothered for as soon as Fadharta had worked out this pattern of events the stones were always back in my field by morning. My father was delighted with our level of activity.

'The lad can work when he wants to,' I overheard him saying. The fact that twelve weeks of strike and counter strike had left the fields in question exactly as they were seemed to bother him not at all, which may explain why he experienced some difficulty eking a living from the rude earth.

The problem was resolved to my satisfaction by a simple ruse which proved beyond Fadharta's powers of understanding. I removed the stones from my field at midnight as was my regular practice. I then went back at two a.m., as wasn't, and cleared his field back into my own. When I returned in the morning, sure enough, the simple fool was standing happily in his field, victorious in his own small mind, surrounded to the tips of his wellingtons by both our stones. I returned with some relief to my reading and both fields remained fallow till the following year.

After this daily simulation of honest toil and the good homely sustenance provided by my mother between her bouts of washing up, I enacted a nightly scene which baffled the poor simple folk I lived with but which furnished me with further raw material for my art. I decided to experience the speech rhythms of the natives in order to transmute the base metal of their speech into the assayed gold of poesy.

Normal procedure is to ascend to the attic and press your best ear to the floor, taking copious notes as you go. This possibility failed to present itself to me as we had no attic, so I climbed up into the rafters nightly and took notes from there. I admit to being a mite self conscious as I was in full view of the assembled throng, which was afforded, in its turn, a full and comprehensive study of the artist at work.

One night was probably much like another but I recall a particularly idyllic scene. Mother was taking a well earned break from her washing up and cutting a new suit for the author from her dress. Father sat not playing the melodeon, turf smoke curling wistfully upwards from his pipe. I remember the conversation very clearly as one of the neighbours had dropped by and observed me scribbling furiously up above.

'Is that fellow a bit odd?' he said, referring to myself.

'He is aye,' said my father.

'He is surely,' said my mother.

My brothers all murmured agreement.

'Was he by any chance dropped on his head as a child?' asked the neighbour.

'He was aye,' replied father, 'but it didn't work for

he was exactly the same afterwards.'

An idyllic scene I grant you, full of a way of life that is long since gone. I can see them still, frozen in time like a yellowing photograph. In many ways a typical family of that era. Father, mother, seventeen brothers, although F.X. was later found to be an O'Flaherty from the Galway Road and Fats was another whose parentage was questioned by some of the more scrupulous neighbours, simply because my mother couldn't remember a thing about him before his forty-second birthday. He used to sit alone at meal times and eat creole dishes of his own making and had a back catalogue of hits from the fifties. He was also black. I can still see them all sitting round the fire, their eyes turned upwards to the embryonic genius in the rafters.

But this is not a linear narrative. I am far too intelligent for that. In one respect, however, I bow to tradition. I refer to the obligatory 'We made our own entertainment in those days' section without which the Irish memoir, however revolutionary in structure, seems somehow curiously naked.

We made our own entertainment in those days. This consisted of my father playing the melodeon. Only when legislation was introduced in 1963 to ensure that every household supplied itself with a television set was this pernicious activity effectively stamped out.

3

The early years of my schooling were overseen by a succession of kindly spinsters, most of whom took early retirement for one reason or another. I remember one lady in particular; Elspeth Funge (Miss) as the newspaper which reported her suicide called her. We knew her simply as Miss Funge or Miss and I'm afraid our relationship was problematic from the start. Miss Funge dealt with us in the patronising way that is common to all primary school teachers. There are those who collaborate with this tendency and I have personally known cases of children who have affected a speech defect in order to gain preferential treatment. Joey the Lisp Adair was rewarded with a regular supply of apples in this way, which supplemented his earnings from an extortion racket outside the school gate.

No fetching lisp nonsense for MacFiach, however. One of my many character flaws is my iron-willed, unyielding integrity. I make no apologies for it. Looked at from another angle, indeed, it isn't a flaw at all but an illustration of high moral character. At any rate it coloured my relationship with the said Funge, who was quite unable to deal with constructive criticism. I well remember our first fracas.

'Now, Fiachra,' she purred in her affectedly unctuous way, 'if I have three apples and I give you one apple how many apples do I have left?'

I was tempted to point out that this was an unlikely scenario and that Joey the Lisp Adair would probably end up with all three one way or another. But I didn't. I merely pointed out that if she couldn't work out that simple conundrum for herself she might be advised to consider a change of career. Harsh words perhaps, but justified, I feel, in the circumstances. My intellectual development appeared to have been entrusted to a half-wit.

Further proof followed within hours of the above. She informed us that she was not one for newfangled notions but would concentrate her attentions on the three Rs. And these were? These, if you please, were reading, writing and arithmetic.

My hand shot up at a speed not seen since the heyday of the Hitler Youth; before self doubt crept in.

'What is it, child?' she said, unaware that her days as our font of knowledge were numbered.

'Reading, writing and arithmetic,' I said. 'That's one R, one W and an A. Phonetically, I am willing to allow, an extra R might be admissible, but arithmetic? I think not.'

I completed my terse if pointed speech with the

observation that her grasp of the fundamentals was sufficiently questionable to warrant a vote of confidence. Not in so many words – I wasn't quite as articulate as that at eight – but she got the message. Her façade of superiority crumbled; she left the profession, and subsequently the world, shortly afterwards.

Mr. Scully was a good deal more robust. I decided to give him a pseudonym for the purposes of this memoir and chose a name at random from the Magherafelt telephone directory (1982 edn). The name I chose was also Scully, but a different Scully. And I have the address and telephone number to prove it.

It cannot perhaps be said that he took an instant dislike to me, because, as I was sitting behind a lumbering buffoon named Brendan Gilhooley, he didn't for some time know I was there. This was certainly satisfactory from my point of view as it allowed me to concentrate on a poem which I was frantically scribbling into my journal against the impending bell.

I blush to recall the work now. I was still in thrall to the tyranny of rhyme and my biographers may detect the influence of Housman (A.E.) in a poem about a cad from Kinnegad who goes to the bad, becomes the victim of a Jihad, changes his name to Vlad and moves to Leningrad. It may be pointed out with some justification that there was no Muslim community in Kinnegad at that time, and my later liberation into blank verse might have been speeded up if I had incorporated a margin note which said, simply, 'Bradford?' But looking back at my journal now (Vol. X1) I see that I was more concerned with the last line.

He was, Mavourneen, but a child.

I crossed that out. Child didn't rhyme with egad. Nor was it a para-rhyme, even if you recited the poem in impenetrable Glaswegian. I tried again.

He was, Mavourneen, but a boy.

Egad/Boy?Worse than useless. I was stuck at this point when the bell rang and it was lost forever, gone to that limbo of the poetic world where unfinished masterpieces pine for completion but trail off instead with a *dot dot dot*.

I may have been upset by the inflexibility of time, but when Mr. Scully decided on a whim to set us a home exercise I sprang to my feet.

'With respect, Sir,' I said, 'the bell has gone. We are now officially outside your jurisdiction.'

For a squat man he moved fast, and with all the natural grace of his simian antecedents. Nor did he pause to explain where he stood on the matter. He simply lifted me from my seat by the nearest available ear and fired me at the partition, his tiny raisin eyes filled with pleasure and hate. As if they had been waiting for just such an occurrence a large group of Christian Brothers appeared at the door – Brothers McKay, McKee, McKinney, McKeown, McCrankey, McCrum, McCroom, McConkey and McCropolis if I remember correctly – and chastised their lay partner with mild reproach.

'Corporal, Mr. Scully. Not capital. Corporal.'

Over the succeeding days, weeks and years Mr. Scully tested the boundaries between those noble forms of punishment. Unacceptable? Perhaps, but the creative artist must suffer for his muse and this, I suppose, was as good a way as any. I was unwilling to say anything about it at home for obvious reasons but my father soon got wind of what was happening. The following morning he donned his best galoshes, marched into the teachers' room and came away, as he himself put it, with some excellent tips.

Is it any wonder, though, that my creative output all but dried up? I spurred myself on by thinking of all those great men in the trenches who pursued their art in six feet of water with rats gnawing at their ankles and only the light of an exploding shell to enable them to proof-read what they'd written. But they were only dealing with the Hun; Mr. Scully was a much more formidable opponent.

Take the following example. During one of the periodic lulls – Mr. Scully busily arranging his underpants over his belt – I was browsing through a recently published slim volume by budding versifier Seamus Heaney. I must say in passing that I admired Heaney at the time for mirroring my own poetic thought if in a more commercialised way, and I was reflecting on the fact that the greeting card industry might be his natural home when a shadow fell across the page. I need hardly add that it came attached to my learned friend.

In moments of stress the mind is known to work on several items of interest at once. In the millisecond it took to divert my gaze from page to face I grappled with the following:

The sad realization that I was about to die unpublished.

The observation that crash helmets should be made compulsory in Irish schools.

The thought that in moments of stress the mind is known to work on several items of interest at once.

I placed my hands over my ears in the hope that my tormentor would experience some difficulty in finding them but imagine my relief on discovering that he had no apparent interest in the left or, failing that, the right. He was standing over the oaf Gilhooley and holding up a magazine dedicated to the celebration of the female form. In a fair world, it must be said, he would have beaten Gilhooley to a pulp. Instead he merely confiscated the magazine and advised the slavering wretch to a) venerate his mother, and b) give all other women a very wide berth.

This advice took the form of a long and rambling dissertation, so I returned to my book. I felt immensely heartened that the author was making a name for himself as the mass appeal of his light verse would undoubtedly lead to greater exposure for his weightier compatriots; to wit myself and, for all I knew, others. I was basking in the reflected glow of this thought when the book was ripped from my grasp.

'Well what have we here?' said the remarkably jocular Scully. He held it up.

'A poetry book, bize. Well excuse me. *Excuzez moi.* I think we all know which side this boyo ties his shoelaces.'

He smirked and winked at his infantile audience, which responded with ribald mirth, then waved the Gilhooley manuscript in my face in an effort to humiliate me further. He suggested that I might like to be referred to in future as Sissy MacFiach and I'm afraid the name stuck for a time, much to the consternation of my Aunt Sissy.

I don't propose to dwell on my schooldays longer than is strictly necessary. I was beaten, ridiculed and, worst of all, forced to play Gaelic games. Now I wish to state, categorically if necessary, that I have nothing against sport in theory, but actually participating is a different matter entirely. It might be said, in fairness, that some sports are worse than others. Rugby, for instance, is a fussy game which interferes with one's ability to write. During a cricket match, on the other hand, I almost finished a 6,000 word essay – on Joseph 'Mary' Plunkett's eccentric habit of playing mixed sex golf with himself – whilst fielding at third man. I would certainly have completed it too if a member of the opposition hadn't wittily (*sic*) unplugged my typewriter.

But Gaelic Games! It has been said with some accuracy that war is a substitute for hurling. This is perhaps to denigrate the former unjustly. And yet I was expected to don a pair of ridiculous shorts once a week and feign pugnacity. My usual solution was to engage the opposition goalkeeper in intellectual discourse with, I have to say, mixed results. The goalkeeper as a breed is noted for stolidity and large hands but not, as a rule, for philosophical agility. On the positive side, however, he doesn't run off when you're getting to the crux of the matter.

And to give goalkeeper Gilhooley his due he was a good listener. He remained crouched in an attitude of mindless concentration as I argued that Gerard 'Manley' Hopkins' middle name was a misguided, not to say misspelled, sop to the cult of machismo. I was interrupted twice in the first five minutes though not, in fairness, by the rapt Gilhooley. No. On both occasions the ball flew upfield in my general direction and, as Mr. Scully was officiating I thought it best to show willing. Twice I took a wild swing at where I imagined the ball might be. Twice it flew past the hapless Gilhooley and between the posts. The effect was immediate and deeply depressing. I became the unwilling victim of a sustained exercise in male bonding, Mr. Scully eyed me with a new respect which I found chilling, and Gilhooley advised me to move away with a neat line in post-war slang.

The long term effect was no less unsettling. As the opposing team struggled to reassert itself Mr. Scully trundled round the field shouting 'Where's MacFiach? Where's MacFiach? MacFiach to the rescue.'

I informed him, curtly, that I was giving the other boys a chance but this had the opposite of the desired effect. Respect turned to adulation. Not only gifted but humble with it.

We lost that game, I'm told, but my unfortunate contribution had been duly noted with the result that I was chosen, to my absolute horror, to represent the school in the year's big fixture. Not having any choice in the matter I resigned myself to my fate and positioned myself within lecturing distance of the opposition goalkeeper.

'Rainer 'Maria' Rilke,' I began. 'Genius or charlatan?'

4

It is not for me to pursue the almost uncanny parallels between the lives of Christ and myself, but I often try to imagine his sullen adolescence, raising his eyes to heaven, for instance, as his mother recounted yet again the divine circumstances of his birth, probably in front of his peers. Adolescence is fraught with danger for the highly gifted and I certainly hope I never have to live through the experience again.

My own adolescence arrived late due, perhaps, to the preponderance of cold winters and I emerged from the experience at the age of twenty seven with my dignity – and clothing – in some disarray. The period in between was perilous. I have mentioned the urge to procreate as one of the great enemies of the artist, but the adolescent knows nothing of this. Nor cares. Nor, I repeat sadly, cares. I have always preferred my hormones dormant but creating the right environment for this is difficult at any age and when age matches shirt collar size it is well-nigh impossible. I recall firing a snowball at a female child when I was six for the sheer pleasure of inflicting pain. The same scenario at the age of twelve apparently denoted love. Such is the frightening fall from innocence.

Sleeping on bare boards has always been a great help to me when I feel a certain sentimentality creeping into my verse, but it was no help in matters hormonal. As a male and an artist I pined for but rejected the lure of the female. In particular I pined for and rejected the lure of Bridie, perhaps the loveliest of the seventeen Gallagher sisters, her slightly crossed eyes and unfortunate ears notwithstanding. We were already linked amorously in the public mind through no act of my own. The parish priest had the tedious notion of joining both our families in stage wedlock for a production of the world's first Catholic musical, Seventeen Brides for Seventeen Brothers.

It closed, mercifully, after a three night run at Oughterard parish hall, but nuptials, whether of stage or life, were not for me. I constantly reminded myself that I was an artist. I was here to observe the world, not to join in. And yet, unfortunately, I was the blameless object of rampant female desire. Women, and before that girls, found me irresistible. I tried wearing spectacles with gaffer tape round the centre. I also developed a nice line in acne and a boil on the left side of my nose which set my spectacles at a pleasing angle. I even went to the extremes of carrying a violin case on my infrequent trips outside but it was all to no avail. I had made a fundamental mistake. I had thrown the snowball of love and Bridie had received it, like Cupid's dart, smack between the eyes.

A woman knows. The snowball linked us indefinably in some way and, while the other adolescents who lounged around the crossroads would tease me as I passed, Bridie was different. True, she called me Sissy and spat at me like all the rest but as she told me later she was just trying to attract my attention.

That I finally succumbed was due in no small part to that other adolescent affliction: the complete absence of a critical faculty. I made the dreadful mistake of remarking to the oaf Gilhooley that the pursuit of wealth was not on my agenda but that I could easily earn a fortune if I was prepared to prostitute my art.

'Take your own field,' I said, my mouth running away with me in my youthful braggadocio, 'the composition and subsequent wailing of the most appalling dirges in the pseudo style of Country and, as if that wasn't enough, Western. Well, even the world's biggest fool could see the commercial possibilities of a song which mentioned every place name in Ireland.'

There. I had said it. He ran off in a state of high excitement. I thought no more about it. Gilhooley, I reasoned, was the type who would never go back to obscurity because he would never leave it in the first place. Wrong, wrong, wrong. Gilhooley wrote the song. He credited me, to my perfectly understandable horror, as co-author. My protests were treated as yet another example of my humility. Is it any wonder that my spots, my broken spectacles, the generous boil on my nose and yes, even the violin case, went for naught? I had

deep probings

collaborated in the composition of a song of such monstrous awfulness that its appeal to the general public was unbounded. I had become, in spite of my best efforts to the contrary, an attractive proposition.

Now there are those who would say 'What's wrong with that?' Precisely this: I have a duty to my reputation as an artist of integrity. I am reminded of the haunting case of Eric Boone. Mr. Boone, I'm told, has spent the past thirty years on the wilder fringes of classical experimentation. His Duet for Noseflute and Mongoose is highly thought of if difficult to perform. And yet in the public mind he is merely the nephew of the man who sang Love Letters in the Sand. Full stop.

I was in danger of a similar fate. My masterpiece lay some way in the future but that was going to be of interest to American academics and, if all went to plan, few others, its wilful incomprehensibility, its multi-layered impenetrability keeping the common herd at bay. Not so my unwitting collaboration with the appalling Gilhooley. Permit me to illustrate my point by printing the first of its innumerable verses.

WHERE THIRTY TWO COUNTIES MEET

I was born in Letterkenny
I come from Castlebar
I hail from a satellite village near Roscrea

Sure I love the girls from Wicklow Town
And the boys from Donegal
As they watch the sun go down on Galway Bay

I'm a Gannon from the Shannon
I'm a Macken from Macroom
And me name is Sean McGinley from Lough Dan

I'm a divil from the Divis flats
A tinker up from Tuam
I'm a cute hoor with a pig farm near Strabane

I'm a Belfast Dublin Kerryman
I'm a Leitrim Longford Derryman
I'm from Castlebar and wherever I may roam

You can meet me here
You can meet me there
You can meet me at the Mammy's up in North Kildare

If I'm in it
For a minute
That's th'oul home.

The name Sissy was quietly dropped. People reserved their
spittle for more deserving cases. If I had composed a great
symphony, painted an Impressionist masterpiece or written
a slim volume of towering genius as, indeed, I was later to
do, the vilification, not to mention the spitting, would have
continued unabated. What does this say about the teeming
masses? The question, I need hardly point out, is rhetorical,
the answer implied in the exasperated, nay world-weary,
tone of voice.

I began walking out with Bridie shortly afterwards.
Bridie liked the song. Inference? We were totally unsuited
to one another. I was an artist and an intellectual, she a
simple country girl whose idea of a good time was a hoe
down and a packet of Kerry creams.

After the initial thrill of my supposed song-writing
prowess – she credited me with sixteen of the thirty two
counties in question – I failed to satisfy her limitless
appetite for dross. The fact that she later married an estate
agent and went to live in the Foxrock area of Dublin
illustrates how low she set her sights, but I was an

adolescent then and knew nothing. I poured my heart out to the poor girl. My hopes. My dreams. My pact with posterity. I spoke to her of dissonance, assonance, para rhyme. She spoke of white dresses, engagement rings, the relative merits of the Maclaren buggy and the Dread-nought pram.

Our total incompatibility must have been obvious to her but she persisted. I have always had this problem with women. They seem to be attracted to the unattainable. I have dedicated my life to art; they sense that. It drives them, frankly, wild with unrequited longing. I recall one particular case where a woman of my acquaintance, on my suggesting that she put me out of her thoughts forever, snorted that I was the last person to be in her thoughts, that I was a dour, humourless bore, an unsufferable prig and a royal pain – not necessarily her exact words – in the fundament. She rounded her speech off by firing a four person cafitière at my head, but I took no notice: I, Fiachra MacFiach, read the subtext.

So it was with Bridie. She became aware that I operated on a higher plane and dropped gentle hints that I might try to lower my sights.

'Wouldn't it be nice to have a good time,' she'd say and, when I'd ask her to define her terms she'd say 'Ah, you know.'

I tried to pacify her with Kerry creams but it was heavily intimated that the same biscuit was part of a broader package – and sitting on a damp wall listening to a disquisition on J.'M'. Plunkett's ambivalent relationship with his half-sister Mary 'Joseph' was not, in her view, part of it.

5

That I pursued the relationship says much for my forbearance, but my youthful inability to keep my mouth shut came into play again with further disastrous results. The nincompoop Gilhooley had taken to following me about like a faithful whelp in the hope that I might supply him with further inspiration for his doggerel. I pointed out that he had covered the country pretty comprehensively and that I could be of no further use to him.

Still he persisted, and not without reason as I was soon to find out. In a state of some frustration I remarked, concerning Bridie, that while I dreamed of art and the immortal verities, she dreamed of the bright lights of Magherafelt. Gilhooley clapped me on the back with admiration and delight.

'She Dreamed of the Bright Lights of Magherafelt,' he enthused. 'Waltz time surely.' And off he went in search of his dreaded banjolele.

deep probings

My eventual split with Bridie was negotiated through a third party. I was summoned to meet her father, a simple rustic type with simple rustic values. I had never previously encountered him but based my all too accurate delineation of his character on the fact that he was a farmer. And to be brutally honest about it I had no desire whatsoever to meet him. Let's face it. A man who spends a goodly part of the morning hours staring at cows' nethers is hardly likely to sparkle on the conversational front after lunch. And yet the pressure from all sides was intense. I was bundled into my best suit. My mother followed me about the place trying to flatten my hair with saliva. My father remarked that Bridie was the pick of the Gallaghers but that I should hold out for six heifers anyway.

'Better still,' he said, 'why not hold out for cash and start a new life in Manchester?'

It was almost a relief to arrive chez Gallagher but I couldn't help feeling that there was a hidden agenda. And so, in the most unforeseen way possible, it proved. I remember vividly standing alone in the living room while the seventeen sisters giggled in the hall. Eventually Gallagher Senior appeared. He strode towards me and, proof perhaps that he was as ill-equipped to deal with the situation as I, he attempted to examine my teeth and hooves. After this initial misunderstanding we got down to the serious business of bartering. That I remained unaware for some time of the objective of the bartering may be divined from the conversation which ensued.

'You've been walking out with my daughter,' he said. I put it to him that I was well aware of this. The man was obviously an idiot.

'Damn your insolence, Sir,' he cried. 'What are your intentions?'

Ah. So he was capable of asking a sensible question after all. Perhaps I had misjudged him.

'My sole intention, Sir,' I said, warming happily to my theme, 'is to write a slim volume of such majestic beauty that the very heavens will open to receive it, and subsequently to bask in the everlasting glow of posterity's approval.'

He was dumbfounded. It was, admittedly, ambitious but, dammit, I had the talent. All I required was time and, as I heavily intimated, less interference from meddlesome bores.

'I demand to know your prospects,' he said.

I stared him full in the face.

'I am an artist, Sir. A genius in embryo. Those are my prospects. Perhaps I could turn the question back on *you*. What are *your* prospects?'

'I work for a living, you insolent young pup. What do *you* do?'

'I repeat that I am an artist, Sir. I write.'

'Do you tell me so? And have you actually written anything yet?'

'Not,' I replied grandly, 'as such.'

'I know the type.' He followed me, not without menace, round the chaise longue. 'So how do you propose to provide for my daughter?'

It was my turn to be struck dumb.

'How,' I gasped, 'do I propose,' I continued, 'to provide for your daughter?' I repeated his words exactly in an effort to locate my bearings. The question was, let's

deep probings

face it, way out there in the stratosphere, beyond fantasy land. I decided to humour the man.

'In a word, Sir,' I said, 'I don't. Does that answer your question?'

He looked at me for a moment. Then he started to laugh. A manic sort of laugh, tinged with lunacy. The seventeen daughters giggled on in the hall. The mother, no doubt, was locked away in the attic, cackling merrily at some private joke. I had stumbled on, almost married into, a madhouse. I still have nightmares about being detained there forever; and when I get to the bit about being an estate agent from Foxrock I always wake screaming.

In other circumstances – if, for instance, her family had been sane – I might have been able to offer Bridie a life of penury. But it was no doubt better this way. The artist is stateless, creedless, and almost inevitably does his own typing. I resolved to have nothing more to do with the pleasures of the flesh. Not that I'd had anything to do with them yet anyway. I had been too busy talking about my plans.

But what was it Burns said about the best laid plans ganging aft aglae? A great artist, Burns, but an appalling typist. What he meant, I assume, was that they often go astray and, such is the universality of his art – at least in Scotland – he could have been talking about me. No sooner had I escaped the lunatic clutches of Bridie and her fellow Bedlamites than I set off for home. My hormones, ignoring the direct route, decided to take a detour past the widow Bernelle's.

It might be fitting, at this juncture, to bring up the vexed question of my sexuality. This, of course, is an intensely private matter involving only myself and yet I sense the unauthorized biographer lurking in the wings, dripping ink. Better, perhaps, to come clean.

The widow Bernelle was a sexually precocious woman in her late sixties. She had moved to the area some forty years previously and the fact that she wasn't a local was held against her in all the usual ways. She would have been burned as a witch but was saved by damp matches. A planned exorcism of her house was cancelled because the parish priest, a vain man, liked his hair the colour it was thank you very much. She was also denied the feminine pleasures of small talk.

Widow Bernelle was swinging on her gate as I passed, a glass of what might have been cold tea in her free hand, a Consulate dangling lasciviously from her lower lip.

'Well hello there, lover boy,' she said, her voice husky from impending cancer. I stood transfixed by her rasping laugh.

'Miss Bernelle,' I stuttered.

She came over and appropriated my trembling hand.

'Less of the Miss,' she coaxed, easing me towards the house. 'Call me Widow.'

I'm not sure what a widow's pension amounted to in those days but she may have been having trouble with her electricity bills. At any rate the living room was bathed only in candlelight. A fire crackled merrily in the grate. A jeroboam of champagne rested on a bed of ice. As Widow Bernelle sat down I heard the rustle of silk stockings. She patted the vacant place on the sofa beside her. I sat on what may have been a wooden foot-stool and watched intently as she poured the bubbling liquid into pink-hued, tall-stemmed, frosted glasses.

A couple of mouthfuls of this heady brew had the remarkable effect of loosening me up and I regaled the widow with bon mots, witty asides and a thorough dissection of the world of poetry and my exalted place therein. She seemed to experience some difficulty in following my thesis, however, if her constant inter-jections were anything to go by.

'You can get iambic with my pentameters any old time you like,' she said at one point and 'Show me your dithyrambs and I'll show you mine.'

Not, I felt, a woman with a firm grasp of the fundamentals, but I ploughed on.

Then, as I recall, she asked me to sit beside her. I declined politely but was immediately struck with remorse. Although a magnificent beauty she was, as I say, in her late sixties and may have been a trifle deaf. I compensated by raising my voice to what in normal circumstances would be regarded as shouting.

Some time later two more bottles of Champagne and the oppressive heat from the fire had taken their toll. I slumped on my stool in a state of no small inebriation. The overheated widow was forced to reduce her outer garments while my lively and stimulating discourse ground to a drowsy halt. Not thinking that I would notice, Widow Bernelle blew the flickering flames out one by one. I had been right about her finances. She even had to ration her candles.

She moved to where I was sitting and began to fondle my top button.

'You must be far too hot in this overcoat,' she

murmured. 'I'm far too hot myself and I'm wearing, why, next to nothing.' She giggled throatily. 'You know what, lover boy? I blame those naughty little dithyrambs.'

I tried to explain that it couldn't possibly have been the dithyrambs, but she seemed more interested in button-fondling at this stage. Having prised open the top one she proceeded to lose interest in it and diverted her attention to fondling the next one down. She was right: it *was* hot. But the thought of sitting there with only vest, shirt and jacket covering my top half made me feel that some sort of response was in order. There were four remaining buttons on the coat. What then? Not knowing what the correct procedure was in such circumstances I began to feel distinctly uneasy.

The situation was resolved to our mutual satisfaction, I'm delighted to say, with a solitary button remaining. She had been fondling for some time and was on the verge of prising.

'I think it's about time we got – how shall we say? – metrical,' she whispered. ' A quick couplet or two never harmed anyone. Hmn?'

I leapt to my feet.

'You're absolutely right', I responded, whipping out my journal and setting to work. She watched in dumbstruck awe as I filled page upon page, guided only by the light of the fire's dying embers.

I staggered out of the house some hours later, rejoicing in the fact that I had come prepared for this most pivotal of occasions. I like to describe an intensity of passion as I go along – a sort of work in progress – even if this means that I miss out somewhat on personal

deep probings

involvement. At sunrise I opened the journal, expecting that the writing would be jerky but legible. Writing in the dark is hardly conducive to excellence in the calligrapher's art, but I needn't have worried. The page was blank. I had omitted to take the top off the pen.

6

It is often said that of all the enemies of artistic promise, politics is surely the most insidious. Who knows what heights Churchill might have achieved if he had refrained from meddling in Germany's plans for world domination. I could so easily have fallen into the same trap myself. That I failed to get sucked into the black hole of making the world a better place was due in no small part to my iron resolve.

Take the following. We had been set the home exercise of drawing a map of Ireland for the great Hibernophile Scully, before the bell had rung this time so there was no escape. I set about humouring the fellow before getting down to my real work, but the coastline of Ireland is composed of the most infuriating mix of inlets, peninsulas, headlands, bays and islands, capes, promont-ories and juttings, seaboards, banks, leas, zigs, zags and squiggles. I had no intention of wasting the whole evening on these absurdities so I made a few minor adjustments. I drew the West Coast when the tide was out and, having spent more than my allotted time getting from Donegal to Dundalk by HB pencil, decided to omit the six counties of the northern state altogether. They were, after all, technically British. In retrospect it took as long drawing the county boundaries. It was refreshing, on the other hand, to get away from the sea.

The map had another fault. My starting and finishing points were the tip of Mizen Head, but the latter ended up several degrees north of the former. That this failed to elicit comment pays tribute to the galvanizing effect of my primary omission. As we stood in line to show our handiwork, Mr. Scully sat on his desk swinging his chubby legs and glancing at each map with yawning indifference. This meant they were traced to perfection. Mine, I thought, was more a work of inspired imagination than a slavish copy. That he remained silent when he first saw it hardly surprised me, frankly. A work of art doesn't yield all its multi-layered secrets at once. But there are pauses and pauses. This, I discovered, was one of the latter. He had merely gone to a place beyond rage. When he returned some time later he was like a man new-born. He set about me with an enthusiasm and vigour remarkable in one of his advancing years.

There was an almost balletic grace about his movements as his squat, long-armed frame swung, literally, into action. I suspect that this is the case with the human animal whenever it involves itself in something it loves doing. And Mr. Scully oozed pleasure from every pink pore. Never, before or since, have I witnessed a living creature so at one with the universe, so totally in control of its own destiny, so illustrative of the dictum that teaching is not a job, it's a vocation. It might be pointed out that my remarkable objectivity in the face of impending doom is almost clinical. To an extent, yes, I would have to agree. But the mind is capable of grappling with several different concepts at any given moment and I was simultaneously able to cope with the following:

The sad realization that I was about to die unpublished.

The observation that small firearms should be supplied to all pupils of Irish schools to help lessen the odds.

I was about to further reflect that in moments of stress the mind is known to work on several items of interest at once when Mr. Scully's brogues hit the floor with a pine-splintering crash. I have never seen Diaghilev dance but perhaps, after all, I don't need to. I stood transfixed, the rabbit to his headlights as he bore down on me, every sinew primed for maximum impact. All thought vanished from my head. I was alive only to the moment. The putrid smell of stale beer and Woodbine. The bead of sweat, with its own private rage, that suicide-bombed the floor. The imminent crunch of bone on bone.

At this point the headmaster popped his head round the door and was about to intercede on my behalf when Mr. Scully showed him the offending, and about-to-be-blood-stained, map. He shook his head sadly.

'Ah no,' he sighed. 'Ah no now. That's going a bit *too* far.'

He gave me a pitying look as I bounced off the partition. Mr. Scully then proceeded with his merry task

deep probings

in the purest state of primal, unfettered joy. Violence, I suppose, just seems to suit some people.

That the above worked to my advantage in the form of a free trip to Derry was due in no small part to the fact that my eldest brother Ferdia was appraised of the situation. A rather morose individual, he blamed everything on 'the Brits'. Bad harvest? The Brits. Extra day to plough through in February? The Brits. I could go on, and Ferdia frequently did. Ferdia had left home to die for Ireland but returned twice a week with his dirty socks. The map incident coincided with one of his visits.

I had grown into a fine young man by this stage, and had developed a pleasingly severe aspect which suggested that I was sole custodian of some deep truth which, of course, I was. I was still some eleven years away from the first flowering of my genius but felt that the time was ripe to chew the artistic fat with my peers. It was time to walk abroad. I donned my best tweed jacket, my scarf and recently acquired fedora, and took possession of my ageing father's walking stick. This would undoubtedly confine him to the house for the duration of my absence, I mused, but the true artist has little room for sentiment. Besides, I had a long walk ahead of me.

Suddenly Ferdia burst through the door, stubbed his toe on the step and blamed the Brits for putting it there in the first place. He then ordered me out of the house at gunpoint. When he was in this sort of mood it was best to humour him so I did what I was told. My parents, I have to say, did nothing. They had been advised that Ferdia's temper tantrums would disappear as soon as he had achieved his aim of a united Ireland and in those days you didn't question the medical profession.

Ferdia had obviously heard about the map. Once outside he informed me that he was going to drive me to the afore-mentioned city where I would spend some time with friends of his experiencing 'the reality of the situation.' There was no point appealing to his better nature – he didn't have one. Nor did he have a car. I contented myself with pointing this out. He looked at me with a new respect.

'Good point,' he said. 'Wait here.'

He disappeared down the road with some traffic bollards and a detour sign. Ten minutes later he was back.

'Hop in,' he shouted. I flung father's stick into a ditch and with a screech of tyres we raced towards the metropolis, a balaclava pulled low over my brother's face against the midsummer sun. Almost immediately we passed a woman with a young child and could, Ferdia supposed, have given her a lift – there was, after all, a baby seat in the back – but as he said himself, 'you never know what you're getting involved with these days.'

As a child Ferdia would regularly lecture me on what he was pleased to call 'the reality of the situation'. He also took me on visits to like-minded folk and, as I knew most of them from school, I often wondered if the blindfold was strictly necessary. He also had an infuriating habit of saying 'When are you going to write something for us?' As far as I knew he wasn't married and I found his use of the royal plural, I have to say, a bit of an affectation.

If the offer of a lift was more than a happy accident, what happened next was proof that I was born blessed. As we approached the city gates I was becoming somewhat

deep probings

apprehensive. What if I had to sit listening to his tedious friends for hour after hour and was left with no time for the business in hand? I needn't have worried. Ferdia had been muttering for some time about the inconsideration of people not filling their tanks and it became necessary for him to drop into a bank near the centre for petrol money. I was pondering my options when a cacophony of police cars descended on the bank, sirens wailing, the officers' moustaches glistening with purpose. The balaclava and gun had turned what was intended as a simple withdrawal into quite an occasion and I wasn't to see Ferdia again for several years.

7

Derry is a vibrant city, in many ways living up to its title as the Belfast of the north. I surveyed it with an almost painterly eye. Its streets. Its portals. Hallowed, for the most part. I wandered about the same streets and, indeed, portals, happily released from the tyranny of dogma. I met a man busking with a lambeg drum and cheerfully placed a small coin in his bowler, although I had to fall in step and take his hat off first. I could afford to be generous. I was about to move among my peers and was reminded, as I strolled merrily along, of the advice given to me some years after his death by poet, playwright and bon viveur W.B. Yeats.

'Sir,' I ejaculated, my ouija board trembling with anticipation, 'I wish only to be a poet.'

'In that case', he chuckled, 'be from Northern Ireland.'

An excellent piece of advice and one that I have tried

to observe to the letter. I further reflected on the subject matter of my forthcoming tête-à-tête with Heaney and began to trawl through my early experience for insights into my genius which might be of interest in casual conversation. I recalled in particular three images from my early youth which established beyond all doubt that I, Fiachra MacFiach, was destined for greatness. I propose to dwell on each image in brief but loving detail.

a. My mother stood with her back to me, her arms threshing about in the sink. Like many women in those days she supplemented the meagre family income by taking in washing up. A fascinating insight into these times can be found in 'Irish Mothers and Other Household Objects', a Catholic Truth Society pamphlet. I also recall that her faded tweed dress had a small gap at the back in the exact shape of my romper suit.

b. As her arms appeared, disappeared and reappeared bearing plates, cups, saucers and the other paraphernalia of the eating process with metronomic regularity my father appeared at the open half door, his back stooped slightly from years of honest labour, the galoshes which protected his wellington boots flecked with frog spawn, a thin trail of turf smoke rising from his ever present pipe.

c. The local constable grunted past on his bible-black, crow-black, midnight-black, head-stuffed-in-a-bin-liner-whatever-the-time-black bike, his giant constable's-uniform-blue buttocks heaving with pleasure.

This trinity of the mind was to stay with me well into adulthood and provide the creative well-spring of my greatest masterwork. But enough of this reverie. There was work to be done. I decided to get down to the business in hand and approached a member of the general public.

'I wish to be directed to Heaney's,' I declaimed, but the addressee appeared not to understand the question. Undoubtedly foreign, I thought, so I decided to rephrase the question.

'Heaney's.' I said, enunciating loudly and with deliberation, 'How much street I go?'

Not only did the poor woman appear baffled by the question this time but seemed, for no apparent reason, rather upset. I removed my hand from her lapel and she scurried off. I was scanning the passing throng for an Irish face when a newspaper hawker said, 'First left, pal. Third shop from the corner.' I thanked the fellow, purchased a newspaper as a gesture of good will and tossed it, and its germs, into the nearest available bin.

I hurried towards my destination pondering what the hawker had said. Third shop on the left. Shop. This suggested that Heaney had an alternative source of income, a wise move in the circumstances. I was pondering the possibility that the emporium in question might well be the city's main outlet for greetings cards when I arrived at the distinctly unhallowed portals.

'S. Heaney – Fishmonger,' it said. 'Wet fish a speciality.' I almost felt sorry for the man.

Apologising mentally to my highly sensitive nose I went inside and yes, the fish was indeed wet. I informed the woman behind the counter that I wished to speak to the man himself and she in her turn informed me that he was outside gutting some cuttlefish and would be back forthwith.

When he finally came in I saw, with astonishment, that he had obviously passed the three score and ten mark some years previously. I've heard of publicity photos being retouched and the like, but the public image of Heaney is, I feel bound to say, flattering in the extreme. The public persona is, I also have to say, a mite friendlier. Heaney in the flesh was glum and taciturn, if not downright hostile.

'I am a great admirer of your work,' I began. He appeared to take no consolation from this but asked me what I wanted. 'Indeed,' I continued, 'I was so taken with your first slim volume that I rushed straight out and bought a pair of wellington boots.'

He seemed faintly irritated. A queue had begun forming behind me, no doubt all wanting him to sign a book or help them out with some puzzling symbolic passage. He asked me again what I wanted. What fish I wanted, if you please.

This is a wily ruse. The artist pretends to be more interested in some mundane activity than in the exalted plane of his muse. It's a defence mechanism and one I propose to use myself when hounded by American academics. So with Heaney. All this talk of fish was merely his way of deflecting criticism, but my fellow interrogators were less persistent than I. They caved in under the weight of his pseudo scorn and pseudo job, contenting themselves with packets of cod roe and the like expertly weighed and packed by the criminally overstretched female assistant.

There are defences and defences, I'm afraid, and Heaney had obviously been stung too often. He persisted with the ridiculous conceit that he was merely a simple monger of fish. But I finally exploded in the face of his false modesty.

'For God's sake, man,' I bellowed, 'I haven't come all this way to discuss fish. I am here to talk about poetry.'

'But I have no interest in poetry,' he objected.

'Then why do you write the damned stuff?' I countered furiously.

'I don't,' he muttered, 'write poetry.'

'Oh all right then,' I said. 'Light verse. Call it what you will.'

By this stage the queue stretched out the door. Who knows what they must have thought of the imbecile. The last straw came when his busybody of an assistant butted in.

'Will I call the police, Stanislaus?' she said.

This was the crowning insult. Stanislaus? Not only was he hiding behind fish, but a pseudonym? This elevated artistic modesty to ridiculous heights. I vowed to have nothing more to do with the insufferable doggerel-smith, bought a half pound of whiting – reduced for a quick sale – and stormed majestically off.

For some days after I arrived home I mused on the implications of the Heaney incident. His cuttlefish-gutting day job may have been a misguided bid for bourgeois respectability. More likely it was a safety net against the almost certain poverty of the true artist. On the other hand, Heaney appeared to have cast off the shackles of his parents – they were nowhere in evidence at any rate – and it seemed to me that the time had come for me to do likewise. I had come to see mine simply as material for my art but it's difficult to mythologize one's parents when they're pottering about the same house.

The circumstances of my leaving were fortunate in the extreme. Throughout adolescence my father would often place a warning hand on my shoulder.

'Whatever you do, Son,' he would say, 'don't go near your mother's chest.'

He was referring, as I later found out, to the metal box which occupied pride of place under the marital bed. My parents, you see, always knew I would be the one to go to university. With peasant cunning they understood instinctively that I was the chosen one – I had certainly reminded them often enough – and so had actually saved up to send me away. Hence the chest.

University is, it need hardly be said, a wonderful place to attend if you want to do something else, and I would often fantasise about the amount of writing I could get done by the simple expedient of avoiding lectures. But which university to grace with my presence? I closed my eyes and stuck a pin in my blood-stained map of Ireland. Limerick. I decided on the best of three, five, eleven, seventeen, thirty one. At this point the pin had landed on Limerick nineteen times, the place where Belfast should have been four times and Monasterevin once. As I knew for a fact that there wasn't a university anywhere near Monasterevin I chose Dublin. I notified the university of my decision. I then wrote to my mother's distant relations, the Dublin Clooneys, informed them that I would be spending three years in their locality and would be pleased to stay with them for the duration. Confirmation, when it came, could not have arrived at a better time.

One of the few remaining pleasures for the older generation is attending funerals and at the time of which

I speak my parents had a couple slotted in. My brothers having gone their separate ways – apart from Fadharta, who was busy rearranging his stones – I was alone in the house. Mother had left sufficient victuals for three days along with directions to the stove. I married victuals and stove and prepared for the luxury of uninterrupted work.

Hours passed. Days? Weeks? The true artist has no concept of time. And so it was on this particular occasion. But however long I had been immersed in my art I was jolted brutally back to the world of affairs by a loud banging on the door. The muse fled. The banging continued. I decided, after due deliberation, to open it and proceeded to do so with barely concealed rage. Outside stood a large crowd of locals. Sweet Jesus, I thought. Mummers. But no. They were merely passers-by who felt duty bound to inform me, if you please, that the house was on fire. And so, on further inspection, it proved.

It says much for my powers of total concentration that a pair of gently smouldering eyebrows – a fair to middling warning to a lesser poet – had failed to rouse me from my work. I was marvelling on this fact, and sharing my wonder with the assembly, when some unlettered lout suggested I contact the fire brigade. This, I'm bound to say, is typical of the peasant class. Faced with the possibility of exploring the mind of genius, they find some excuse to return the subject to the mundane, the everyday.

It is not for me to speculate as to how the fire started. Ferdia blamed 'the Brits' and it certainly bears all the hallmarks of a politically motivated act, the consequences

deep probings

of which could have been tragic in the extreme. My parents, on their return, were thrown on the mercy of the state, not having any alternative accommodation or, for that matter, money. Fortunately, however, I was leaving anyway so the inconvenience was minimal.

The postman arrived that afternoon with a letter from my uncle.

'You'll be the parasitic psuedo-poet who killed his brother,' it began. A fine example of mordant Dublin wit, no doubt, but humour is a luxury of the idle class and I was a busy man. I pocketed the letter unread.

As soon as it was safe to do so I went inside to collect what remained of my belongings and I must say I was sorely tempted to sue the fire brigade. In dousing the flames they had completely soaked my work in progress. A blank notebook, I grant you, but they weren't to know that. On a happier note I went to the remains of my parents' bedroom to claim my inheritance. My mother's chest being impervious to fire I pocketed the not inconsiderable sum it contained, bade farewell to my youth and headed south.

8

I am, to my almost certain knowledge, the only undisputed genius of the MacFiach line. Great Uncle Alisdair found fame of sorts as drag artiste Sweet Alis MacFiach while my distant cousins Joel and Ethan Clooney received an Academy Award nomination for Best Short Film by Identical Twins. But, even if we count the latter as one unit, the term genius seems curiously inappropriate in this case. Cinema is, after all, a minor art form, closer to basket weaving or balloon sculpture than to my own lofty pursuit.

It was arranged on my arrival in Dublin that I would stay in the twins' room – Joel and Ethan being away at film school – and that I would pay my way by tutoring cousin Rosemary when not engaged in my own studies. My uncle's wife – my aunt – had gone to live in a women only commune in Borris-in-Ossory and my uncle, when not away on business, would sit around the house drinking heavily and weeping.

deep probings

Cousin Rosemary, the youngest of the Clooneys, was by common consent exceptionally beautiful although I must say that I find baldness in a woman, whether by accident or design, singularly unattractive. It was perhaps understandable, then, that Clooney père saw fit to lecture me on matters of propriety regarding his only daughter. He took me to one side and informed me, a steadying hand on my shoulder, that Rosemary was 'getting to that age'. Not knowing what age that age was I decided to humour him in his cups, and said that I was delighted to hear it.

He wept into his glass for a seemingly endless moment before embarking on a maudlin homily. The odd phrase and word hit home. 'Like her mother.' 'Salacious.' He tried this one several times till he got it right. The other word that stood out was fornication and his concluding burst – 'If anyone so much as lays a finger of lust on my daughter he's a dead man. I have the contacts.' – was delivered with fire, passion and clarity. He concluded by saying that Rosemary was particularly weak at algebra.

I resolved to begin her lessons with Transsexual Subtextuality in the Poetic Output of J.'M.' Plunkett. But first there was the small matter of settling in. Joel and Ethan's room was a shrine to cinema. They had often stayed at my parents' house as children and I well remembered them getting me to stand watching them, in all weathers, in the field at the back of the cow shed while they checked camera angles and lighting. Such dedication to their admittedly populist art was reflected in the books, posters and film scripts that lined the walls of my study to be.

I cast a cursory glance at their various projects. This

was not mere idle curiosity on my part. I had overheard them speaking, on one occasion, about their desire to find a subject that would encapsulate the complexity of modern Ireland. I had coughed politely in order to draw attention to myself and they had both appraised me for some time, falling silent in the process. In the hope that I had thus inadvertently planted a seed I rifled through their effects.

I discovered in passing that my eccentric cousins weren't the only family members involved in this most ephemeral of art forms. A two-reel biopic from the silent era charts the historic occasion on which Joseph 'Mary' Plunkett represented his country at tennis. Plunkett, apparently, was the mixed doubles team. Great Uncle Alis won two Oscars for the part – the first time Best Actor and Actress had gone to the same person – but this, of course, still doesn't make him a genius.

I was about to give up on my search when Aha! A folder marked Work In Progress containing several likenesses of myself captured over the years, interspersed with requests for funding for a 'serious' film based on a 'genius'. Vindication! The seed had, indeed, been planted. I put the folder to one side and surveyed the rest of the room. Posters, books and boxes of cinematic trinkets dominated the small space. Impossible for a poet to work with such distractions it goes without saying, but such was the depth of their collection of mindless trivia, with the obvious exception of the folder, that it took me several days to bin the lot.

My university career, by this time, was over. It had been shortened somewhat by my failure to register for any course, a fact which had upset the bureaucrats. I had

deep probings

decided on history as my main subject – as a way of contextualizing myself – and in the opening lecture revisionist historian Professor H. Doody developed his thesis, I believe, that the Great Famine coincided with an almighty surplus of chocolate biscuits. As I had more important matters on my mind, needless to say, I decided to give it a miss. What if the muse should strike while the professor was busy pontificating? If my experience of that pompous breed is anything to go by it would have been well nigh impossible to shut him up.

No, I decided to head straight for the library which was, to my intense annoyance, full of nervous students busily taking notes. The fact that examinations were only nine months off no doubt explains this, and there wasn't a seat to be had in the place. I stood to attention for some time, weighed down by the tools of my trade. Notebooks. Poetic texts. Scarf. A young woman eventually vacated her place. Others were waiting alongside but I was the hungry one. I got the seat. The woman in question had left some of her possessions on the adjoining desk. Books. Purse. Flask. Reading glasses. A couple of bags. Lunch box. As a helpful gesture I bundled these on the floor in a neat pile and set to work. Some minutes later she returned, muttering furiously to herself, collected her belongings and skedaddled without so much as a thank you. I remember reflecting at the time that to mislay a biro suggests a careless nature. But books? Purse? Flask? Glasses, bags and lunch box? And talking to herself? This suggested a mind on the borders of sanity so I wilfully ignored her in case she decided to embarrass herself further.

I had only just set about my work with a will when it became apparent that I needed to visit the lavatory. I left my book open, scarf draped casually across my chair. Inference? I'll be back. And so it must surely have been obvious to any rational human being, but Ireland at the time was going through one of its periodic two hundred-year cycles of religious hysteria and was overrun by nuns; most of whom, I regret to say, were in the library at the time.

My books, on my return, had been placed on a nearby trolley. My scarf was folded neatly on the floor. And in my place? Yes. A nun. Now I am not a violent man, but her vow of silence limited the option of rational debate. My aforementioned belief that war simply suffers from a bad press came to the fore.

The Irish legal system, however, is weighed heavily in favour of the Church. As far as I know it's still illegal to hit a nun. The next best solution, I decided, was psychological warfare, so I stood behind the chair and read over her shoulder. This form of mental torture is renowned for its effectiveness and, needless to say, some hours later she vacated the seat and the library was left to darkness, as the poet Gray so judiciously put it, and to me; and, it must be said, the janitor, followed, well before midnight, by a couple of burly, moustachioed security guards and, the following morning, by the Machiavellian intrigues of the college bureaucrats.

My truncated scholastic career confirmed me in the belief that third level education is the civil service of the mind. Some days later I applied for a fellowship at the same university and my failure to get the post reinforced

deep probings

my theory that the true artist is always an outsider.

My speech to this effect, I'm afraid, was somewhat lost on the afore-mentioned security guards who escorted me to the gate, and my parting comment that if ever I found them starving to death in some wretched hovel they would get no chocolate biscuits from me was met with the vacant smiles of the happily foolish.

The artist-as-outsider speech may have failed to move my audience but it had an electrifying effect on me and I lost no time in expounding my views to cousin Rosemary during our next session. Not wishing to appear boastful I referred to myself in this context only in passing, but confined my thesis to the outsider status thrust upon Joseph 'Mary' Plunkett in spite of his excellent marks in the civil service entrance exam. Cousin Rosemary sat rapt with attention, drinking in my every word. All too soon, however, the lesson came to an end and she closed her algebra book with a pleasing demureness. Mathematics is not a girl's subject, granted, but she was a bright student and would, under my guidance, do well.

9

In many ways, as I say, an idyllic time. The master-pupil relationship ripened into something deeper. Lecturer-audience. The sole blot on our intimate sessions was the constant interruption of her increasingly inebriated father. The pattern, if disruptive, was at least predictable. He would insinuate his head round the door, stagger in and motion me to one side. There would follow a supposedly confidential man-to-man with a hand placed heavily on my shoulder to help him remain upright. Rosemary, he would begin, was getting to that age. I replied, on each occasion, that I was delighted to hear it. He would then weep into his glass for a while before embarking on his bombastic, and seemingly eternal, set speech. The odd word and phrase hit home – but 'salacious' presented a regular problem, interrupting his thesis which was, essentially, to warn all would-be suitors off on pain of imminent death. A brief reference to algebra would

deep probings

conclude the proceedings and off he would slope to nurse his secret sorrow.

I describe the above because a later confrontation suggested my personal involvement in his drink-induced vision. We had positioned ourselves to one side as was the regular practice. His hand was on my shoulder. He had forsaken his habitual tumbler of whiskey for the decanter, and was more inebriated than usual. On this occasion I couldn't understand a word he said but I was, after all, his guest. We were speaking man to man. I knew the ground rules.

He slurred his opening gambit.

'I am delighted to hear it,' I replied when silence reigned.

He wept into his decanter for a while. I stood there wondering what to do if the muse should strike. Then he was off again. A pause.

'I'm sure she's the image of her mother,' I replied, 'but not being on intimate terms with my aunt I hardly feel qualified to comment.' There followed a disjointed ramble which appeared to include variations on the letter 'S'. This, too, eventually ground to a halt.

'Salacity is indeed a state best avoided,' I averred.

He then placed his decanter on the nearest available surface, released his grip on my shoulder, raised himself up to his full height and inserted his thumbs into his waistcoat, a model of sudden sobriety.

'I am delighted to hear you say it,' he said. 'But I put it to you that it is not this child who is guilty of salacity, you young blackguard, it is you. I put it to you that it is not this child who is the hunter, you adolescent excrescence, it is you. I further put it to you, you libidinous voluptuary, that you have defiled this child with your lecherous eyes and come hither manner. Know this: I abhor your impudicity. I repudiate your carnal concupiscence. I heartily forbid your concrescence. And as for your lustful concubinage, you low cur: Nip it in the bud. Forthwith. Because also know this: I have the contacts.'

So saying he strode to the door and slammed it dramatically in his wake. I was outraged. This drunkard, this dipsomaniac, this sot, had dared to accuse *me* of leading other than a blameless life. I stood trembling with wrath. The door opened. He reappeared, clutching a fresh decanter.

'By the way,' he slurred, leaning against the jamb, 'she's particularly weak on algebra.'

Despite these regular interruptions, however, our daily lesson ran smoothly and, as I often made it my habit to take the afternoon air it seemed inevitable that Rosemary should join me on one of my walks. A mistake as it turned out, but the experience began agreeably enough. Bearing in mind the statistic that in ninety seven per cent of traffic accidents in sunlight there's a bald pedestrian nearby I stayed well away from the road, and cousin Rosemary matched me stride for manly stride in her twelve league army boots.

All went well as we set off from the house. All was fine as we turned the corner down to the seashore where Brian Boru had famously pitched his tent in 1014. Locals are still bitterly divided as to whether he had a valid permit and I was about to observe that we Irish are still steeped in old battles when I noticed that cousin Rosemary had become distinctly agitated. We were passing the main gate of the local convent school at the time and there she parked her boots, a defiant look in her wild adolescent eye.

I was about to develop my thesis tangentially when a member of the religious order approached the gate and this led, it pains me to report, to the wildest torrent of vilification I have ever encountered between one human being and a nun. I have since located most of the expressions in a dictionary of north Dublin street cries and am only dissuaded from quoting her impassioned speech word for word by the expectation that this memoir will eventually become a standard text in secondary schools in the English speaking world.

Cousin Rosemary's basic thrust was that the sister in question was a _ _ _ _, a _ _ _ _ _ _, and a _ _ _ _–_ _ _ _ _ _.

'You abused me as a child you _ _ _ _,' she elaborated. 'You are a _ _ _ _ing _ _ _ _, a _ _ _ _ing _ _ _ _ _ _, and a _ _ _ _ing _ _ _ _ing _ _ _ing _ _ _ing _ _ _ _.'

The sister in question, who appeared to be black if her face was anything to go by, stood less than two feet away and a conversational tone, to my mind, seemed more appropriate.

But cousin Rosemary ranted on regardless. A crowd began to form comprising both lay and religious. The Mother Superior appeared. A caucasian lady of indeterminate age, she shook her head sadly.

'Don't be silly, Rosemary,' she said. 'Sister N'gola has spent the last forty years with the missions in darkest Africa. You really are the most appalling fibber.'

Cousin Rosemary trembled with rage.

'I'm going to have a child by an intelligent man before my sixteenth birthday you _ _ _ _,' she snarled. 'So _ _ _ _ you.'

Mother Superior pressed her fingers together in an attitude of prayer.

Rosemary thrust her arm through mine and held me as tight as a car clamp.

'Come on, lover,' she spat. She strode off down the street and I followed helplessly in her wake. As we reached the corner she turned and gave Mother Superior an aggressive salute.

'Rome sucks, _ _ _ _ _.'

I didn't catch the reply.

I tried to put the above scene out of my mind by returning to the subject of Irish history. I even broadened it out to include a dissertation on my place in it but my thoughts were elsewhere. I tried to think of some way of extricating my arm from that of my libidinous cousin. *I* was an intelligent man. Rosemary was obviously aware of this. She had also referred to me as 'Lover'. This posited a potentially explosive and time-consuming scenario. But I noted that the further we got from the convent school the less the pressure on my arm and after half a mile or so I was back in control of my own destiny. I kept a wary eye out for any other convents, just in case, but the moment had passed. Peace of a sort descended. My monologue proceeded undisturbed.

We walked along the promenade for a while and shortly cousin Rosemary decided to return to the parental home, no doubt to make notes of what I'd been saying. I was not unrelieved. I had spotted a couple of distant figures in black waddling towards us, bibles aloft.

The day and I were hot. The sky and sea were blue. I decided to purge myself of my recent trauma by immersing myself in the cleansing waters of the salty main. I walked along the strand for some time until I had left the world of people behind. I removed my clothes and laid them neatly on the sand. I placed my work in progress beside it. I toyed with the idea of bringing the precious document into the water with me but felt that this would unduly restrict my movements. I wished to merge totally with the life force. To become one with the universe. To float free of the mortal state. Besides, I would only be gone for thirty seconds.

I ran to the edge of the sea and, with a whoop of joy tempered somewhat by my natural reserve, tested the water with my toe. I pondered my options. It was certainly colder than I had expected. I was beginning to feel curiously undressed and the gulls' cries seemed, in my present state, to have turned to mocking laughter.

It proved, on closer inspection, that it was indeed mocking laughter which assailed my ears; not of gulls, however, but of small boys. I caught a brief glimpse of them as they disappeared into the sand dunes with my clothes. They seemed highly amused by their action but it's rare for the victim of ridicule to laugh heartily at his own humiliation unless there are television cameras present. I was about to give chase when I noticed that my work in progress remained where I had put it.

They had taken my clothes but left my notebook! This was beyond humiliation. I was mortified. The notes were mainly random – aphorisms, bon mots and the like – but there were also fragments of verse. Did they not like them? I imagined them flicking through the pages and being unimpressed. I was devastated. These insecure thoughts, typical of all great artists, lasted but a second, though, before my rational mind took over. They were, after all, mere children so giving chase would be futile. I could never have hoped to explain my working methods. I might, on the other hand, have got my clothes back.

This left me with the problem of returning chez Clooney, a distance of some two miles through a hostile bourgeois landscape, in a state of total undress. I could have waited till darkness and clambered over back gardens, but the sight of a naked man negotiating garden walls in the dead of night is open to misinterpretation, even in these liberal times. I decided, instead, to brazen it out. If I walked along as if fully dressed, I reasoned, the chances were that the broad mass of people would accept that I was, indeed, in that happy state. How wrong I was.

I had intended my arrival back at the Clooney residence to be discreet. It turned out to be anything but. I was seen down the drive by a crowd of well-wishers and pubescent girls on bicycles, and was about to tip-toe round the back when the front door opened and Mother Superior ushered me serenely in. She gave me a beatific smile and averted her gaze at her leisure. I followed her inside and closed the door with relief.

Père Clooney was waiting for me in the living room and I have to admit that, on the surface, things looked pretty bad. I was expected to give cousin Rosemary her daily grind at five thirty and it was now well past six. But my uncle had other things on his mind. He was also remarkably sober.

deep probings

'Come in m'boy,' he said. 'Brandy? Cigar?'

I demurred. I was about to suggest that I run upstairs and find some clothes but he seemed agitated. Best, perhaps, to indulge the fellow.

'On second thoughts,' I said, 'perhaps just a snifter.'

I helped myself to a havana and we smoked and drank for some hours in silence. Cousin Rosemary sat demurely on the sofa, eyes downcast. Mother Superior smiled beatifically beside her. In many ways I was glad she was there. A woman about the house, even one with a fixed beatific smile, exerts a civilizing influence and Clooney responded accordingly. He exuded geniality where before had been tetchiness, harmony where before had been conflict. I found myself warming to the guy.

'The thing is, m'boy,' he said eventually, 'Dublin . . .'

'Ah yes,' I said, beginning to feel, by now, the mellowing effects of the brandy, 'Dublin. City of Joyce; Beckett; Johnson, Mooney and O'Brien.'

'Yes yes,' he replied testily, ruffled slightly, perhaps, by my superior knowledge, 'never mind about that now. The thing is, m'boy . . . It's not really you, is it? You being an artist and all that. Solitude. That's what you need. Somewhere quiet to jot down the odd limerick. Eh?' I could see that he would never understand the soul of a genius but he had struck a chord. 'One of those uninhabited islands off the West Coast now,' he continued. 'That'd be just the ticket. Away from all those distractions, d'ye see. My . . . how's her algebra, by the way?'

I ignored the question, rhetorical I fancy, and looked at the man with a new respect. I sighed wistfully and poured yet another large brandy.

Mother Superior coughed beatifically. My uncle looked startled and weighed in afresh.

'The thing is,' he said, 'I have the tidy sum of five hundred pounds here – Irish money – that says yes! Your dreams *can* come true!'

I was flabbergasted. Here was a man who had every reason to believe that my intentions towards his daughter were not entirely honourable and yet his main concern was to subsidize the arts. I looked at the notes in wonderment.

'Five hundred pounds!' I said.

Mother Superior shifted beatifically in her seat.

'Offer him six.'

My God! Religion and Art in happy union at last! Huzza! My uncle grappled with the new figure.

'Six hundred pounds!' I said.

Mother Superior's smile broadened and set.

'Did he say six? He meant seven fifty. Didn't you, Mr. Clooney?'

My uncle grappled with the new figure.

I laughed, involuntarily, with delight. Mother Superior stood beatifically up.

'Nine hundred,' she said. 'And that's his final offer.' She extended her hand. 'Let's shake on it.'

My uncle produced his wallet with trembling hands and peeled off the required number of notes. He looked not unemotional as he placed them in Mother Superior's free palm. Without extricating her hand from mine she flicked her commission from the top and passed me my six hundred pound cut.

'It's more than worth it, Mr. MacFiach,' she beamed.

deep probings

'You are, after all, a most intelligent man.'

Rosemary blushed demurely from the sofa. My uncle downed a celebratory tumbler in one.

'Nine hundred,' he slurred. 'Jesus Christ! I was quoted eight fifty by a hit man.'

I failed to see what that had to do with supporting the arts but was pleased to accept his generous gift and found myself, some forty minutes later, deposited on the Galway road with sufficient victuals for a light lunch, a large sum of money in my back pocket and the screech of my uncle's tyres in my ears as he executed a u-turn and roared off home.

10

I began my journey west in a state of no small inebriation. In mitigation I merely point out that I am an artist and while it has never been adequately proven that sobriety harms the creative faculty, it's hardly worth the risk of finding out. My uncle had very kindly supplied me with a road map which suggested, mistakenly, that the main route to the western sea-board was one way. It also seemed an excessively long journey so, at the next petrol station, I bought a smaller map.

But time was of no consequence. I was a free spirit, unburdened by the cares of the world. In spite of my noticeably handsome features and easy charm I had managed to ward off the attentions of the women of Ireland with almost laughable ease. I was shortly to embark on a relationship, however, which tested my steely resolve to snapping point and almost caused me to betray my great gift.

I was passing a field at the time. Oh, it was much like any other field. Flat. Stone-encrusted. Enclosed by dry stone walls and a metal gate over which peered an ass. Her long, mournful face followed me as I shuffled wearily along, my light lunch long since eaten. One of her forebears had borne Christ in triumph into Jerusalem, but I was thinking only of easing my weary feet, as we could hardly expect the same type of reception in Athlone.

I opened the gate and motioned her out. No response. I doubt if the Bible goes into detail about this bit, but an ass is not noted for its obliging nature and this particular one had a generous helping of the relevant gene. I was on disagreeably intimate terms with her rump before I gave up and marched off in disgust. As soon as I was gone she trotted happily out of the field and followed me down the road.

It is often said that the ass is the most loyal of animals if a mite unwieldy as a house pet, and this particular model was no exception. We exchanged what may have been a bonding look. All the more unfortunate, then, that several miles down the road I spied a second ass both younger and fitter and managed, after a good deal of effort on my part, to engineer a straight swap. This may sound like an easy enough task but the first ass didn't want to go into the field and the second ass didn't want to come out. After much jockeying for position and the best part of a bag of carrots I found myself standing in the road with both asses in the field, staring at me over the gate as they munched carrots. Half an hour later I had both asses where I wanted them but I was eating the carrot. It was nearly nightfall before I had the situation finally resolved. I read some days later that the new owner of my old ass had his entire stock destroyed because of a contagious wasting disease traced to the same poor beast. Lucky swap.

I was right about Athlone. No flower-strewn paths or shady palm trees. Just the odd honk from an irate motorist as we negotiated the town's labyrinthine traffic light system. And so on out to the West with its rugged terrain and matching people. I decided to give the ass a name. Assumpta. It is perhaps only when we leave Ireland that we fully comprehend what a ridiculous name Assumpta is, but Assumpta wasn't to know that. Besides, Assumpta the Ass was pleasingly alliterative. It had the ring of a children's best seller about it, although I was damned if I was going to lower myself to that level of hack work.

Assumpta proved a stout friend and a wonderful listener. The odd braying noise merely acted as a pleasing counterpoint to my discourse. It was as if she was saying 'Do you tell me so?' or 'Pray continue, fellow. You interest me strangely.' As with all the best travelling companions my subject matter was wide ranging, my treatment of it witty and informative in the extreme. I spoke at length, for instance, on the subject of book titles. Eminent Neanderthals. Urdu the Hard Way. And that paean to conscientious objection They Died With Their Slippers On. None of which, by the way, I had read.

No. I confine my reading to the poetic arts. I live and breathe great poetry and it was while remarking that one of the benefits of a Catholic education is that it introduces us to doggerel we would not otherwise have read that I was struck by an excellent idea. The bards of

deep probings

old would ply their trade from house to house, enlightening the inhabitants in return for full bed and board. The Rhyming Priest springs to mind as an excellent example of this genre, although his subject matter was somewhat limited.

> It's much to be prayed for that one day the Pope'll
> Convert the poor people of Constantinople.

Fine as far as it goes and rhythmically sound, but take, then, the following:

> I hope that the Pope, that good friend of the Celt,
> Will convert the poor heathens of Magherafelt.

Or, indeed:

> I pray that the might of the Vatican See
> Will convert the vast hordes of the heathen Chinee.

Vast hordes I like. Vast hordes is good, but the Rhyming Priest was in many ways a victim of his own success. He hit upon a winning theme and milked it to death – his own in this particular case. His decision to crack Belfast was ecumenically sound but he ended up on a Shankill Road bonfire after taking bad advice.

My decision to follow in his exalted footsteps was not taken lightly. I am not by nature an exhibitionist, but my speech accepting the Nobel prize for literature would demand certain performance skills. Projection. Clarity. The ability to feign humility. It was no bad thing to start practising on the peasants of Connaught. Having established that Assumpta would remain out of sight until

I had a foot in the door I rapped boldly on the first house I came to.

'I am an artist,' I declaimed. 'I demand sustenance in return for which I will entertain you with verses to delight the mind.'

I discovered, in the course of such visits, that ninety per cent of Irish homesteads possess at least one shotgun, usually loaded. But I am an artist, not a market researcher; I merely pass the information on.

11

My luck seemed set to change as I negotiated the winding, pitiless mud tracks of Connemara, after a chance meeting with an itinerant musician of my acquaintance. I refer to Blind Cearbhúil O'Dowda, an uilleann piper who hails from the stony vicinity of my parents' old home. His pipes could often be heard over the intervening bog if the wind was from the north. Or, for that matter, from the south, east or west; and my father professed himself an admirer.

'That Cearbhúil has a lovely tone,' he said once. Cearbhúil, at the time, was in Australia. My father's critical appraisal coincided with some of the local children winding a tom cat through Mother's mangle. An understandable mistake. I, too, often thought I heard my father squeezing a tune from the dreaded melodeon when, in fact, his mother was dying of consumption. But Blind Cearbhúil, and his mournful pipes, were a special case. As soon as I heard that high-pitched wailing tone I knew who it was immediately. Two musicians like that, my admiring father used to say, and the country would sink under the weight of misery.

I reached the brow of the intervening hill and there, in the distance, a fire blazed, joyful in the act of burning. Two figurines sat round it, Cearbhúil and a female companion who, on closer inspection, turned out to be that mythological hardy annual, the snaggle-toothed old crone. A dying breed, sadly, in these days of improved dentistry and skin cream. A not unattractive blend of methylated spirits and horse manure wafted up from her person and she beckoned me to sit.

We passed a pleasant time swapping verses and stories, the more depressing segments highlighted by Blind Cearbhúil's melancholy wail and Assumpta's attendant brays. This fine old tradition was given a thorough workout through the evening hours and we were being entertained by one of Blind Cearbhúil's interminable airs when Assumpta became suddenly restless. Blind Cearbhúil stopped pumping his bellows, a remarkably considerate gesture to a dumb but suffering animal. The music trailed off some time later.

'There's a crowd of people coming,' he said nervously.

Hmn, I thought. A classic case of stage fright. Fine with a couple of friends round the camp fire, but give him a real audience and he disintegrates. MacFiach, on the other hand, rises. The crowd may have been attracted by the lure of the pipes and the fire, but they were heading, without knowing it, towards more elevated fare. This was a golden opportunity to test my latent verse speaking skills.

They were still a good way off, which gave me plenty of time to prepare. I set to work sifting. A hint of Plunkett, naturally. A soupçon of Yeats – as an accessible build up to my own greater complexities, I hasten to add. Heaney? Certainly not. I was still bridling from his ridiculous subterfuge and the growing suspicion that he might even have short-changed me on the fish. My programme was still a tad light. Blind Cearbhúil had lost his nerve. I would, by the look of things, have to go it alone.

I decided, therefore, to compose a piece especially for the occasion and, opening a notebook and untopping a pen, waited for the muse to strike. Time being at a premium I was concentrating intently and not without desperation when Cearbhúil stood up.

'No doubt about it,' he said, 'they're definitely coming this way.'

He commenced gathering his belongings together in some haste, as did his lady friend. Very well then. I would face the challenge solo.

The necessity of carrying the evening on my own stimulated my endeavours. The sky was clear. The fire was bright. If I could seize the moment the symbolic resonances would be profound. This, people would say in years to come, is the spot. I, they would continue, was here. I began to have great plans. In this very place, I decided, I would start the MacFiach Summer School. Readings. Seminars. Doctoral theses from obscure Mid Western universities analysed and dissected in the bars which would spring up around the event.

From this it was but a short leap to MacFiach Night. Robert Burns was in great demand, while he lived, on

Burns Night, and the same would apply to MacFiach on MacFiach Night, which would be held annually on December the twenty fifth, his birthday. I was thinking of the increased sales of my work generated by this event – with a spin-off industry in mugs and key rings – when I was rudely interrupted by Cearbhúil.

'Are you coming?' he screamed at me.

I most certainly was not. There was too much at stake. But at least he'd jolted me out of my reverie and back to the business at hand. I continued to trawl the subconscious depths of my teeming genius. What may have been seconds or millennia passed. Then! Hallelujah! The Muse! I pounced on the page, scribbling furiously and emitting sounds which seemed to well up from the pit of my stomach and demand to be heard. I had been consumed by a great vision which might have run to volume upon volume had I been granted the gift of solitude. Three words, however, were all I was allowed before Cearbhúil, that damned interfering busybody of a blind piper, shook me violently.

'Are you mad or what?' he yelled.

'Not yet,' I replied with venom, 'but when I am, you infuriating pedant, you'll be the first to suffer.' Harsh words, but fully justified in the circumstances. The unthinking fool had killed a masterpiece at birth.

He and his fancy woman looked suitably startled, then fled like mice before the scythe when our prospective audience marched into view. I was destined to face them, on this historic occasion, alone. I stood to greet them, sans masterpiece, and heard one of them shout, as they were still some distance off, 'We'll have no dirty oul tinkers here.' It's *thinker* I sighed inwardly. *Th. Th.*

I was painfully aware, of course, that the word tinker exists in its own right, meaning itinerant, gipsy or even, in certain dictionaries, tramp. This linguistic clarification took but seconds and was followed, crisply, by three concurrent thoughts:

That it might take longer to explain this to my approaching guests.

That the baying sounds and wielding of cudgels suggested a possible antipathy to intellectuals.

That three thoughts can coexist happily during moments of impending death.

With seconds to go I leaped on board Assumpta and she stumbled resolutely off into the surrounding darkness. As a final gesture I tossed my aborted masterpiece in their wake. It was, in its present form, of no further use to me.

12

I naturally abandoned all thoughts of a summer school on that particular spot but at least I had escaped with my life. In fact, not only was I alive but I was rude with joie de vivre. The sun was now shining. A fresh breeze brought a tang of the sea. Trotting along beneath me was a beast which had saved my life. I was also in excellent fettle because Blind Cearbhúil, before his attack of nerves, had alerted me to the possibility of opening my bardic account several miles down the road.

Briefly stated, Blind Cearbhúil had been admitted to the house of one Gerret. And as soon as Gerret heard Blind Cearbhúil playing he had begged him, for a generous fee, to perform for his close neighbour Gunter, whose birthday it was. Blind Cearbhúil had immediately made his way to the latter's house and was greeted with some hostility. Gerret and Gunter, it appeared, were involved in a bitter feud. Blind Cearbhúil happily pointed out that Gerret was obviously extending the hand of

deep probings

friendship in a gesture of conciliation and, in order to advance the peace process, he had played for several hours.

My own plan was a variation on this theme of conciliation. I would go to Gunter's house. Keen to return the compliment and cement the relationship, Gunter would naturally employ me to perform my aborted camp fire programme for Gerret. Who knows, the barriers might come down and Gunter's daughter marry Gerret's son, or vice versa. Assuming, of course, that such people existed.

I negotiated Gunter's elaborate security system and was soon outlining my plan to the master of the house. As soon as Blind Cearbhúil's name was mentioned he began to tremble with emotion. He let out a stream of expressions in German, some of which – Donner und Blitzen, Ach got in Himmel and the like – I recognized from the boys' magazines of a bygone age. His wife calmed things down somewhat with a riding crop, and I was able to proceed with my idea. Blind Cearbhúil had hardly been successful in his stated objective of uniting the two houses but I was certain to do better.

Gunter calmed down, as I say, and listened to my plan. He asked for an example of my work and, in the absence of a stage area I leapt onto a coffee table and declaimed from there. Two lines into a rendition of Horace in the original school syllabus Latin he rubbed his hands together in glee and begged, nay, commanded me to stop.

'Splendid,' he said. 'This is just the way to repay my neighbour's fine if misunderstood gesture,' and, emboldened by a cheque from the Bundesbank and Gunter's almost childlike desire to achieve a lasting peace, I made my way round to Gerret's.

Gerret listened earnestly as I explained the situation. He expressed himself touched in the extreme, but had what he thought was a better idea. He was still deeply upset by the failure of his original plan. What if he doubled the amount given by Gunter? Would I be willing to go back and try again? During these elaborate negotiations, Assumpta, whose taste in food is catholic in the extreme, was calmly eating the sofa.

On the basis of this brief account of my trip I fully expect a commission for the obligatory travel book. The route from Dublin to the West may not have the romance of, say, Newtownmountkennedy to Cadiz, but unlike certain parties I have a fine eye for detail of place and, more than that, my relationship with Assumpta had developed, over the long days of my wanderings, into something uncommonly deep and spiritual. My journal entries around this time display signs of maudlin sentimentality which have never, of course, seeped into my verse. I poured my heart out to that dear ass in a way that I have found possible with no other man, woman or beast of the field.

She was much more intellectually curious than Bridie, with an ability to walk past nuns without erupting which contrasted pleasingly with cousin Rosemary. No. Assumpta loved, honoured and, on a more regular basis than the modern female of the human species, obeyed. The ideal mate, in many ways – if only she could have typed.

And here I must stifle a sigh. For we arrived,

deep probings

eventually, at the broad Atlantical ocean. Opposite us, my new island home, where I might yet write my masterpiece. Behind us . . . what?

I began to see that the island represented the artistic impulse, while Assumpta, sadly, stood for domesticity, a nine-to-five job and constant worry about the price of oats and hay. And yet oh! the agony of loss. The people brushing past on the narrow quay. The captain barking orders. The moon lighting up the mournful expression on Assumpta's long face. True, she looked mournful even when dancing one of her periodic jigs, but behind the plaintive expression on this occasion was a new and unbearable grief, a black sadness at the heart-breaking inevitability of it all. The inexorability of fate. Her instinctive understanding that I was destined to follow my muse.

'Go,' she seemed to sob. 'Go. Leave. Get on that accursed boat. I . . . understand.'

The engine chugged into life. The captain barked a final command. I left Assumpta on the quayside and climbed aboard the boat that would take me out of her life, forever. Assumpta stood, silent and impassive, and watched me as I left, her long, languorous face and melting eyes cutting me to the quick. The boat chugged round the headland and out of sight but I kept watching as her feet, body, neck and finally her long and melancholy and still languorous face slowly disappeared until all that remained were the pointed tips of her majestic, ever-attentive ears.

> Methought I heard her mournful bray
> But 'twas only the wind in the rigging.
> *(Old Song)*

13

I recently offered my journals to the classics department at the university of Alabama in return for an honorary doctorate but was curtly informed that if I wanted an honorary doctorate I could pay the $100 administrative fee like everyone else. They offered a doctorate of Divinity at a knock down $50 'while stocks last', but not wishing to enter northern Irish politics as a psychopathic Presbyterian I didn't see the point.

The relevant journal is, therefore, still in my possession, and the section dealing with my island adventure affords a penetrating insight into the creative mind.

> THE ISLAND JOURNAL OF FIACHRA MACFIACH.
> I
> Arrived, at last, on island. Accommodation spartan – small attic room above MacAdoo's public house; rent in advance – but by pressing ear to floor can experience speech rhythms of fine old Gaelic

deep probings

community. Decide to learn Gaelic. To immerse myself in the culture of my antecedents. Tonight, however, rest. Boat over a tug. Squat. Black.

II
Spent morning unpacking. Paper. Pen. Complete Plunkett (J.'M'.) Several anthologies (Verse). Spare scarf. Wad of notes.

III
Grappled with muse. Medium: verse. Subject: tug. First line:
A squat, black tug . . .
At this point muse fled. Writer's block. Spent hours on line, rejecting
A squat tug, its colour black . . .
There was a tug, a squat, black tug . . .
Both lack resonance.

IV
Asked MacAdoo for name of good Gaelic teacher. Recommended himself. Demanded money. Gave him week in advance. Phrase learned today: *Buíochas le Dia ta alán airgead agam*: Thanks be to God I have a lot of money. Repeated phrase for MacAdoo. Doubled rent.

V
Rejected
A squat, black tug . . .
Line now reads
O squat, black tug . . .
Other plans for day scuppered.

VI
Spent morning with ear pressed to floor. Experienced racing from Haydock Park.

VII
Frustrating day leafing through Collected Plunkett (J.'M'.). Verses about tugs – nil. Later same p.m. wandered abroad. Mud road led to other mud road. Other mud road led to boat slip. Squat, black tug bobbing on water. Looked distinctly unpoetic.

VIII

Second lesson. Phrases learned: *Bhfuel tabhair dom é más ea*: Well give it to me so. First conversation in Gaelic.
Myself: *Buióchas le Dia ta alán airgead agam.*
MacAdoo: *Bhfuel tabhair dom é más ea.*
Excellent progress.

IX

Ear to floor. Experienced old Audie Murphy Western. 'Routine oater' – I. Times.
Scoured anthologies. Favourite topics for verse: spring; death; mothers. Least favourite: tugs.

X

Third lesson. Phrase learned: *Go bhfóire Dia orainn, táim skint.* God's curse on it I have no money.
Repeated phrase for MacAdoo. Given notice to quit.

XI

Spent morning packing. Paper. Pen. Complete Plunkett (J.'M'.). Several anthologies (Verse). Spare scarf. Loose change. Pressed ear to floor for last time. Experienced early Norman Wisdom comedy. 'Strictly for the fans.' – *I. Times.*

XII

Met MacAdoo on tug. Going on extended holiday. Unexpected windfall.

XIII

Back on mainland. Decide to abandon tug verse.

IXV

Inspired by muse.
Medium: verse.
Subject: mother dying in Spring.

XV

Writer's block.

14

I left Ireland an embittered exile. It was the done thing. No further explanation should be required for this. Embittered exile is, after all, an ennobling thing in itself. And yet there were practical reasons for my decision. I entertained the not unfanciful notion that Bridie might try to sue me for breach of promise. Besides, my parents' present circumstances ruled out a return to the landscape of my birth. The prospect of sharing a dormitory with them and who knows how many other ne'er-do-wells had a certain romantic appeal but I would hardly get much writing done.

A return to Dublin was also out of the question. Oh, I had no doubt that my relatives would be pleased to see me. The ties of family are hardly loosened by the passage of time. No, I had more professional reasons for my principled decision. I mentioned, some time back, my application for a fellowship at Dublin's Catholic university.

Not having heard anything on my travels I resolved to revisit my old campus. They might have been desperate but unable to contact me, although I'm sure a brief television news flash would hardly have upset the few remaining fans of Audie Murphy or, for that matter, the decadent aficionados of Racing From Haydock Park.

At any rate, I was working my way back to my alma mater with visions of a lifetime of wine and cheese when fate chose embittered exile over the soft option of academia. I was cutting a swathe through the stones of Westmeath when three people ran from the ruins of an ancient castle, remonstrating wildly. As the first two got into their car the third party, a man in a suit, charged after them, frantically waving a newspaper at them.

'No no. You're thinking of 'Ideal for first time buyers'. The ad distinctly says 'Would suit D.I.Y. enthusiast'.'

He flung the paper to the ground in disgust and stormed off. A gust of wind ruffled the pages and one of them blew across my face as I marched along. The following headline hit me at eye level: Nun Awarded Fellowship At Dublin's Catholic University.

Now I am not a pedantic person. Far from it. I am also a feminist to my fingertips. But consider this, I had applied for a position as a fellow. Now a fellow, unless I am much mistaken, is a man. So 'pedantic'? I think not. And yet. . . this was a sign, surely: Get out, MacFiach. Now. Your work is elsewhere.

And so it was that some days later I found myself sharing the night boat with those poor unfortunates unable to make a living in their homeland. My journey, it need hardly be added, was geared to an altogether more glorious purpose.

And it is perhaps appropriate that I wrote the bulk of my masterpiece on that night boat to England. It was as if the physical break with my roots had unblocked my genius. I spent the entire journey writing furiously, oblivious to all around me. And, at the end of my epic voyage, there lay Ireland on paper.

I will deal with my working methods elsewhere. Suffice it to say here that the first poem was out almost before we had lost sight of land. Lines For Seamus Heaney operates on fourteen different symbolic levels, some of which I myself don't understand, although an American doctoral thesis will no doubt enlighten me, perhaps posthumously, to the awesome nature of my own profundity.

Why Lines For Seamus Heaney? To be honest I pitied the man. I'm not sure a fishmonger lives on after the last person who's eaten his produce. My generous gesture will at least ensure him a footnote in history. I reprint the work in full on the strict understanding that it acts merely as an appetizer to the full slim volume.

> The gnarled tree explores
> The muddy field,
> Its lecherous roots probing
> The wet, brown clay
> Like the gnarled and crackling fingers
> Of a tough, old, two-quid whore.
>
> My father's gnarled spade
> Impales the ground
> With a soft, sensual, sucking sound.
> His bent back,
> Old and gnarled, shields the spade
> Like cupped hands over a butt-lighting match.

A gnarled toad squats, croaks,
Leaps and lands
Beneath my father's downward thrust.
Spade and toad meet
Like the inevitable consequence of something
                              almost tribal.

Frog lies squelched beneath blade.
My father pulls at the gnarled wood of the spade,
The ground sucks
And all is as before.
The gnarled tree.
The probing roots.
The clay-sucking spade.
And deep in the wet, brown clay
The once quick frog.

Still.

Silent.

And probably still gnarled.

15

A lesser poet would have stopped there and disappeared to the bar, but not MacFiach. I merely glanced around to check where I was before giving further vent to my art. Opposite me sat a couple with a young child. The energy had been sucked out of them by their horrendous offspring, who forced them to attend to his every whim. I glowered at the brat as he smeared chocolate on his comatose mother. He burst, gratifyingly, into tears. I set about Further Lines For Seamus Heaney and forgot all about the wailing minor in the joy of creation.

The verse in question obviously reads, now, as if it had always existed. But not so. It was wrested from the very depths of my soul and I was midway through the penultimate line when tragedy struck. My biro ran out. I was distraught. What to do? I looked wildly around. Most of the passengers were hidden behind piled up crates of cheap Australian lager. The couple opposite were indulging in that curious half sleep that always expects to be woken. Their charge had been bought off with a colouring book. He was working at the time on a circus scene, his child-sized face puckered up in concentration, a black crayon in his podgy little fist. I gathered up my belongings, double checked the aforementioned parents, grabbed the crayon with a lightning raid on his unsuspecting hand and was half-way to the door before the wailing resumed.

It was a wild night on deck but I managed to finish what was perhaps my most moving lyric to date: Further Lines For Seamus Heaney. If the child responsible for supplying me with writing materials is reading this, may I just say 'Congratulations! You have not been born in vain.'

The lyric will become, I fancy, my most requested piece at readings. Four words in and the remainder will assuredly be drowned out by sustained, impromptu and heartfelt applause.

> My mother's plump hand . . .
> (SUSTAINED APPLAUSE)

The written version will proceed as follows:

> . . . grips the neck
> Of the plunger. Water
> Swirls and squelches
> Slops
> Plops and sluices.
> The plunger plummets,
> Hammers home with a plump slap
> And sucks itself stuck.

My mother heaves.
Strains.
Throbs.
The plunger taunts. Hard.
Erect.
Clamped.
My mother, stung, grits her gums,
Pulls
And PLUCK! – the plunger unplumps with a slurp
and a suck.

My mother, spent
Sits, sighs and sleeps.
I watch her wilt and sag,
Her bulges droop
And in her sleep
She softly
Plumps her blubber.

It will no doubt shock my many admirers to learn that this enduring opus was almost consigned to the depths of the Irish sea. As a preparatory exercise I decided to map out a first draft on a separate sheet of paper. I naturally keep a copy of all drafts filed away for my official biographer's use. But as I say it was a wild night. No sooner had I written the title and jotted down a couple of disparate images than the sheet of paper was ripped from my hand by a gust of wind and flew overboard. The only other person on deck was a young man of impressionable age. By his size and general demeanour I took him to be an athletics student at a minor American campus.

'Quick,' I cried. 'Grab that!'

Startled by my obvious passion he leaped across the handrail and disappeared heroically into the night and the pitiless sea. The paper, I'm afraid, was lost forever. I managed to forge an almost perfect facsimile for posterity but am bound to report that it lacks the fire of the original. And the loss of that historic document wasn't the only negative aspect of this unfortunate incident. I used the word heroic to describe the young man's exit. This was not strictly true. As he flew over the side he appeared to have second thoughts, not being fully aware of the import-ance of his gesture. At any rate he took a wild lunge at my wind-swept scarf which unravelled from my neck at an alarming speed. He thus went, without nobility, to join the afore-mentioned document in its watery grave. As far as the paper is concerned I accept a certain degree of resp-onsibility, but the impetuous young fool must shoulder full blame for the scarf. On a happier note, my arrival at the poem's final full stop and the boat's arrival in port coincided to the second. A thrilling end to an historic voyage.

The trip to London was less stimulating. I was motioned over to a table by a customs officer having prepared, in advance, a witty riposte to his inevitable 'Have you anything to declare?' My bold reply would mark me out from my fellows as a first rate mind. It would amount to a declaration of my genius and of nothing else. This witty riposte would be passed on by word of mouth, quoted in one of the more salubrious broadsheets and eventually traced back to its self deprecating author. I cleared my throat in readiness. The customs officer eyed me balefully as I emitted a hearty chuckle.

'Would you mind opening your bag, Sir?' he said. I replied – I can't recall the exact words – that I wouldn't mind in the least, Officer. An appropriate answer, certainly, but hardly the stuff of legend. His fault, I feel, for denying me the appropriate feed line.

deep probings

The train journey augured well. I appeared to have the good fortune of sharing a carriage with an American couple. I had always thought of Americans as happy-go-lucky, fun-loving and outgoing, but this couple were glum in the extreme. Catatonically glum. I began to look on their countryfolk in a new and more favourable light. A few more like these and I'd consider living there myself.

The peace was shattered, however, by the arrival of the chocolate covered couple, their offspring still in tow. No sooner did he set eyes on me than he began howling in a most offensive manner. I tried losing myself in my work but it proved impossible. The child wailed on and appeared to do so without pausing for breath, much like a human bagpipe.

Such are the times we live in, I'm afraid, that I was powerless to respond. I was in a supermarket once when I was approached by a woman who screamed 'I cannot abide people who smack their children.'

'How dare you, madam,' I replied, 'they're not my children,' but I have since treated children, and small people generally, with delicacy.

'Now now, Justin,' said the father, 'that's the gentleman's crayon.'

I mean good God. You don't reason with a three year old. Fortunately they got off at Wolverhampton and apologised with an ease born of obvious practise. I waved them away magnanimously but the little blighter tried to jump from his mother's arms and claw at the window as they passed outside. He had succeeded in totally shattering my concentration and moments later I tossed his damned crayon in the bin, contenting myself for the remainder of the journey with adding to the prevailing mood of towering gloom.

I should have kept it, of course. It did, after all, write a masterpiece, but my letter to British Rail to this effect some weeks later received the following reply:

'Dear Mr. MacFiach,
We regret the loss of your half-used child's black crayon on the Holyhead-London service last month. Not having a precise day of travel we double checked every train used on that particular route to no avail. Cleaning staff are trained, naturally, to spot items of cultural importance in the waste bins and you may be assured that a few heads have rolled over this incident.'

Good thing too. We arrived at London Euston several hours later and, as we got off, the male half of the American couple broke what I had taken to be a vow of silence.

'For the last time, Martha,' he growled, 'I thought he was with you.'

Observing my look of distaste – I was with neither of them – the gentleman saw fit to explain.

'Pardon me, Sir,' he said. 'It's our kid. He's gone awol and boy are we mad.'

A brief description of the 'kid' in question showed him to be none other than the scarf-snatcher of ill repute. The totally unnecessary loss of said scarf had begun to fester by this stage and I treated his ex-parents to a terse, if minutely detailed, synopsis of the events leading up to its loss. By the time I had finished I was seething with anger. I demanded – and got – monetary compensation.

A spare scarf, admittedly, but it could so easily have been otherwise. They both wept for the wrong they had done me and I left them with the pointed observation that if people only considered the problems of others it might help to put their own in perspective.

16

My time in London flew by. This was borne in on me by my brother Francis. I was staying with him and his estimable wife Philomena when one day he came into my study and coughed politely. Some two hours later I finished what I was doing and gave him my undivided attention.

'Fiachra,' he said, 'your original plan, I believe, was to stay for a couple of weeks.'

'That,' I replied, 'is substantially correct.'

'Well, that was three years ago.'

I have to say I was flabbergasted. Three years? Why it seemed like only, well, a couple of weeks. I thanked him for keeping me up to date on these matters and suggested that Philomena might like to bring me a cup of tea when she had a moment. I then returned to my work.

Not for the first time I was distracted by loud noises outside.

'He'll have to go,' shouted Philomena at the top of

deep probings

her voice. A good woman in her way but one of the Birkenhead Begleys. In that particular locality voice projection is a necessary tool of survival. But this 'He'll have to go' business. She often said it, always at the top of her voice and I could never quite figure it out. Apart from myself, Francis, herself and her first child – whose name escapes me – there was no-one else there. Curious.

Philomena might often appear to the outsider to be coarse and aggressive but she understood the importance of art. No sooner had I arrived than I gave her the first draft of Lines For Seamus Heaney as a belated wedding present. Yes! The original copy! Admittedly it looked like a verbal bomb site, but I'll bet the Bible looked pretty ropey before it was typed up. So this historic document was intended as a very special offering indeed. That she was aware of the fact was plain from the disbelieving drop of her generous Liverpudlian jaw.

Imagine my horror then when she failed to have it framed, as I humbly suggested, and put in the place of honour over her mantelpiece; where the middle flying duck presently flew. Days had passed. No sign. I eventually confronted her with my puzzlement. What was the problem? Where, in a word, was it? My sister-in-law positively exploded.

'Where is it?' she cried. 'Where is it? It's in the British ruddy Museum is where. You don't expect us to keep a valuable manuscript like that on the premises! Think of the insurance!'

Her speech was peppered with colloquialisms but the gist is in the above. I stood corrected. I had grossly misjudged the woman.

My first task was to find a publisher and I posted some carefully selected samples of my work to Faber and Faber. What followed gave me an insight into the world of publishing which suggested that I might experience difficulties getting my genius recognized. Faber, it appeared, liked my work. Faber didn't.

I had entered the rarefied world of the book publisher, where pap is rewarded with a bloated advance while genius is left to fester with its mentally unstable sister-in-law, penurious. There was nothing for it. Necessity dictated that I approach an agent. There was something about the term bloated advance which lost its negative implications when Philomena was in full flight.

Not being au fait with the breed known as agent I was unsure of the correct procedure in procuring their services, so I got hold of a book with the misleading title The Compleat Letter Writer. Compleat? It was nothing of the sort. The selection was arbitrary in the extreme. Example: 'A woman has given birth to fifteen children by artificial insemination and wishes to thank the rugby club which donated the sperm.' No less than three different approaches to the problem with a generous selection of rugby clubs to choose from. Encouraged by this seeming inclusivity, I looked up the section Genius Wishing To Procure Services Of Agent. Nothing! I was, it would seem, on my own. I returned the book to the library with a curt note in luminous yellow on the frontispiece warning other readers of the yawning gap between title and reality, then got down to business.

My introductory letter to an agent chosen at random described the agent class, approvingly, as the midwife of art.

It mentioned that advances running into millions seemed to be the norm these days but that I, as a first time poet, would be happy to settle for slightly less. I toyed with 'considerably less' but didn't want to come across as an easy touch.

Not receiving a reply by return of post I decided to drop by. Put the chap at his ease, so to speak. My bullish ambition has a habit of overwhelming people on paper but meet me in the flesh and all melts into camaraderie and banter. And so it proved. I stated my business to a menial and, on being told that the agent was busy, stated with some emphasis that I too was busy but had allocated the next half hour for the business in hand. She bowed to my iron will and pressed the intercom.

'There's a Mr. MacFiach to see you,' she said. A pause. 'I told him that but he seems, well, quite insistent.'

He, too, bowed and some thirty seconds later I was ushered into his office.

'Well,' I said. 'What do you think?'

He backed away slightly, cowed, perhaps, by my penetrating gaze.

'What can I say?' he said.

'I have no idea.'

This, it need hardly be said, was an untruth. He could obviously have said that I had written a work of genius and that he had spent the morning alerting the publishing world to the brightest star in the artistic firmament. Modesty in the face of my gift is, however, one of my less attractive flaws. I held my peace.

He seemed agitated, and began surreptitiously fingering the contents of his waste bin. Without doubt a sick man but that was his problem.

'MacFiach,' he mumbled. 'MacFiach.'

He seemed to be searching for the apposite phrase, so I leaned across the desk to spur him on.

'I presume,' I said, 'you saw what I was trying to do.'

'Trying?' he said, startled by my forthright manner. 'Trying? More than trying, MacFiach. You've succeeded triumphantly. Having said that . . .'

'You don't think it's too dense?'

He waved my question away. 'On the contrary.'

'What?' I said. 'Not dense enough?'

I knew damned well it was dense enough but I was testing him. Why choose the wrong agent when I could have my pick?

'No no,' he said, fearful of losing a prospective client of no small prestige. 'Spot on in the density department. Perfectly dense. Not to mention' – he seemed unnecessarily sycophantic at this point but I could take it – 'densely perfect.'

I sprang to my feet.

'I'm delighted to hear you say it. It's just that fourteen different symbolic levels can tend to overwhelm the first time reader.'

'Fourteen?' he said.'Twenty at least. Possibly more. Who can tell?'

I chortled wryly and made some witty comment about the artist not fully understanding his own work. He sighed dramatically and lamented the fact that he had a full roster at the moment, that he wished one of his clients would die and that his secretary would see me out. I chose to ignore this. I gave him the hard MacFiach stare. Almost a glare to some ways of thinking but a look that pierces, at

deep probings

any rate, soul to soul.

'And which,' I asked, 'was your favourite piece?'

He looked suitably alarmed at the magnitude of the question but gave an answer, after an interminable pause, which pleased me greatly.

'I can honestly say,' he said, 'that they all stand, at present, absolutely equal in my eye.'

I could work with this man.

'I am delighted by your answer,' I averred, thumping the table that now stood between us. 'But we must sacrifice one to the press. Strictly for publicity purposes. You know the sort of thing. One of those boxed items in the obscure hinterland of Saturday's Irish Times. A message to the reading public: 'Le nouveau MacFiach est arrivé.' I paused. 'Which one?'

He leaned across the table.

'To be brutally honest, MacFiach,' he said, 'your work is so deep, so resonant, operating as it does on such a multiplicity of levels, that you cannot possibly expect to be published in your own lifetime.' He marched to the door. 'I am humbled by your genius.' He opened the door with a flourish. 'You write for future generations, MacFiach. Make no bones about that.'

For one in his exalted position to recognize the claims of posterity on my work is beyond high praise. I left his office in a state of euphoria, his parting words resounding in my joyful ears as I feigned nonchalance and strutted gaily to the exit.

'Come back in two hundred years, MacFiach,' he thundered. 'We'll clean up.'

17

Armed with this positive response I set about my work with renewed vigour, uninterrupted by the mental instability of my now-pregnant sister-in-law. I mention the pregnancy because it interfered with my epiphanic decision to perform my work in public. I remember the occasion well. I had taken to walking the streets of London for the purpose of kick-starting my muse and had just sent an old gentleman sprawling on the footpath. London is a city of some twelve million people and it's nigh on impossible to avoid them all. He had the good grace to apologise for creasing my notebook and went on his way in a state of some confusion. On the ground where he had fallen, among the debris of this mighty city, lay one pair of dentures, a pacemaker and, more to the point, that day's edition of an English broadsheet open, fortuitously, on Other News.

'Heaney Helicopter Tour,' it said.

It seemed that the once-bashful bard was to use the proceeds from his fish sales to fly around Britain reciting to the masses. I closed my notebook and rushed home. I couldn't afford a helicopter, of course. No fishmonger I. But Francis had a car of some description and this would do to be going on with. As if reading my mind he was about to unlock it when I arrived.

'Excellent fellow,' I said, climbing in the back to avoid conversation. But what was this? Ye Gods! Philomena was already in there, fondling her large stomach and moaning softly. A quick jaunt in the country was the last thing she needed and I made the point with some force.

'No no, Fiachra,' said my brother, 'it's her time.'

'*Her* time,' I said. 'What about *my* time? Look.'

I pointed skywards. A helicopter hovered overhead as if to taunt me.

'That . . . impostor,' I said, 'has got a head start already.'

It was no use. Francis, normally the gentlest of men, ordered me to vacate the car immediately. I did so. I've heard of outsiders coming in and destroying close families and Philomena was a stunning example. So be it. I, Fiachra MacFiach, am an artist and above such trivia.

I raced round the back and grabbed hold of a rusty bike which had been lying there for some years. I leaped aboard and started careering down the street, the helicopter still hovering overhead, taunting, taunting. I had gone perhaps a mile when I was struck by the sudden realization that I had no money, no publicity, no venues, no dates – and my poems were back at the house. I also appeared to have a puncture, no lights, and the unsolicited attention of a passing police car. I dismounted and walked home, resolving to be better prepared next time. And wouldn't you know it? The car was back before me. 'False alarm', apparently. I said nothing, but this *'her'* time' codology was in danger of scuppering my career. Without realizing it I spent the following two hours scowling at Philomena as she watched her women's programmes. Francis tried to lighten my dark mood by insisting that the helicopter circling overhead was merely monitoring traffic. I didn't believe him at first but then spent the rest of the evening and most of the night writhing in a state of steadily increasing outrage. Not only did the appalling Heaney have a thriving fishmongering business and a healthy income from the light verse circuit. He was also 'coining it' in his spare time with a job in traffic control.

Naturally enough I wrote to the same man suggesting that he was taking unfair advantage over earth-bound poets. I further suggested that he might care to support my cause with a direct debit. Not that as a genuine artist I was in any way interested in money, but Francis and Philomena seemed unhealthily obsessed with the stuff. Overdrafts. Mortgages. The price of prams. As a result I tried to steer clear of them as much as possible, but a private income would enable me to steer clear of them full stop.

Emboldened by my letter to Heaney I had even decided to solicit funds from other sources and made a list of possible benefactors, when Francis approached me for a 'quiet word'. Money, with Philomena pregnant again, was a terrible problem. They might have to consider renting out the spare room. This was fine by me, I said, but I suggested that Francis have another look at the layout of the flat. As far as I knew there wasn't a spare room. I'd be more than happy, however, to help him look. Francis went away with a chastened look and a loud wailing sound from the living room shortly afterwards proved my point. They had obviously bought the property, mistakenly, as a three bedroom flat.

What with all this talk about money and Philomena's increasing hysteria it became nigh on impossible to work. Things quietened down a little when Francis took a part time night job to supplement his meagre clerical salary. But Philomena, at this time, was nine and a half months pregnant and almost intolerable to live with. On the slightest pretext she was off to the hospital and my witty remark that she must be having an affair with one of the orderlies was received in stony silence. An admission of guilt, perhaps? I resolved to breakfast on my own in future. I also resolved to keep my personal affairs to myself following a rather revealing incident at the same repast.

The post had just been delivered. Bills for Francis, a personal letter from Ireland for myself. Francis, who had earlier bridled at my suggestion that he should get more sleep, stuffed his letters irritably in the toast rack. He watched with apparent fascination as I opened mine. After staring at the missive for some moments, I gasped in disbelief.

'This,' I spluttered, 'is an outrage. This,' I continued, 'is outrageous.'

It is possible from the above outburst to guage my feelings precisely. My normal fluency had given way to a faltering outburst of variations on a single phrase. My mind's eye swirled with exclamation marks.

'Listen to this,' I cried.

Philomena woke with a start and removed her face from the butter dish.

'My dear Fiachra,' I read, 'how's she cutting?! Well, Where Thirty Two Counties Meet really done the business all right! Plus! She Dreamed of the Bright Lights of Magherafelt is hot off the presses! What a team! Go aisy with your cut! Any more ideas?! Yours Truly, Brendan!'

The imbecile was trying to implicate me in his appalling musak. This could destroy my reputation before I even had one. My position in history was in the balance. I grabbed hold of the enclosed cheque therefore and tore it to pieces, a series of noughts across the front of it swimming before my eyes. Francis shook his head slowly and walked to the door. Philomena burst into tears and sank back into the butter dish. Both had seen the integrity of the artist at work and responded as each saw fit.

18

I fired off an irate letter to the dunderheaded warbler advising him as to what he could do with his 'Yours Truly' and it was, perhaps, not coincidental that this outburst of ire was followed by a period of total concentration on my work. I was masterful, filling page on page of my journal with taut and supple prose. That same evening I became pregnant with the muse. Rejoice!

The true artist is born in a state of married bliss. He, or, in a smattering of cases, she, could hold out an edition of his collected works and say 'I'd like to introduce you to my wife.' Perhaps not – I tried it once with odd consequences – but the implication is clear. It is impossible to devote one's full attention to family life *and* art. Permit me to illustrate the point.

Francis was rounding off his working day with an evening shift at Ward's Irish House. Fact. Philomena was heavy with child. Fact. I was pregnant with the muse. Fact.

Francis was out. I was in. Philomena was about to give birth. Fact. Fact. Fact. You begin to see the broad picture. Because of my brother's inability to control his own affairs I had been cast in the role of in loco husbandis. Philomena decided her time had come. The normal rules of civility – not her strong suit in the best of circumstances – deserted her in their entirety at this juncture. She burst into my room.

'Get me,' she demanded, 'to the hospital. I'm dilating.'

In artistic terms so was I but consideration for others is not Philomena's strong suit so I held my tongue.

'Can you drive?' she said. I was about to explain my feelings about driving under the influence of genius but she cut across my opening word.

'Then call a taxi, please.' This, at least, is the doctored-for-schools version. Her actual words were muscular and forthright but by this stage I'd had enough.

'The hospital,' I said, 'is within easy walking distance. It's a beautiful night. Let's go.' And, grabbing hold of my notebook and a couple of spare pens, I marched on ahead.

Philomena followed. She had no choice actually as I'm damned wilful when the mood takes me. And the mood was certainly taking me here. We hardly spoke en route. To be brutally frank I felt a bit hard done by. My mind was full of conflicting thoughts and images. My muse. The brusque response of Ward's Irish House to Francis' request for pre-natal paid leave. The fact that I was wrong about the proximity of the hospital and the weather. It rained all the long, long way.

Now I am not, I think, a difficult man to deal with. My needs are simple, my expectations few. But I hope I

deep probings

am never forced to write another poem in a hospital. Medical staff, be they doctors, nurses or people with mops, seem congenitally incapable of remaining silent or standing still. Hither and thither they rush without any apparent thought for others. I was, as I say, heavily pregnant with the muse and, true, I gave birth to a masterpiece later that night. But I did so in spite of the most appalling intrusions.

My previous experiences of waiting rooms have taught me that they are nothing but breeding grounds for the worst type of bore, so I accepted the nurse's offer of accompanying Philomena to the birth room. She seemed unwilling to engage in banter – we hadn't spoken since leaving the house – and this suited my purposes admirably. I laid my journal and notebook down at the end of the bed and set to work with a will. I was making excellent progress when Philomena began uttering the most extraordinary noises and calling loudly for her mother, who was in Birkenhead at the time. I managed to ignore this for a good while, confining myself to the odd 'Ssssh'.

Matters took a turn for the worse, however, when the nurse started to fuss about the room, talking to Philomena in a very loud voice although Philomena by this time seemed in no fit state for conversation. Then the nurse, a large girl from Galway, turned her attention to me. It might be worth considering an epidural, she said. I must say I found this vying for custom distasteful in the extreme. Besides, I wasn't there to be tampered with so I politely, if a trifle frostily, declined.

Work, at this stage, was achieved under the most extreme duress. Philomena began to direct a stream of abuse at me that was totally uncalled for. She then broadcast a series of personal details for anyone who cared to listen. I was a pompous, insufferable, priggish bore. I was – I can hardly bear to write it down – a fifth rate scribbler of verse with delusions of mediocrity. I had a mole on my left buttock. Naturally enough I was absolutely furious.

'Now look here,' I said, intending to put her straight on the verse business, but at this point the nurse came back and cut across my speech.

'Ah sure they're all like that with the ould husband,' she said. 'It's a sure sign the babby's on its way.'

'Damn your impertinence, woman,' I replied testily, 'I am not her husband.'

This, for some reason, struck her as having humorous intent.

'That's a good one all right,' she chortled, her large Galwegian frame rippling with mirth.

As soon as she had left the room I gave Philomena a stern lecture on her obvious lack of training in literary criticism but she started screaming that it was coming and I was reminded of what I was doing there in the first place. I took my chair over to the corner of the room and was delighted to discover that she was right. Within hours I had produced, without fuss or personal abuse directed at a single innocent third party, what may well stand as my finest achievement to date. I am referring, of course, to Yet Further Lines for Seamus Heaney. I went home shortly afterwards and slept for twelve full hours, exhausted by my miraculous fecundity.

I reprint it here in full, safe in the knowledge that

deep probings

readers not yet in possession of Deep Probings will want to read it twice.

> The constable cocks his leg,
> Heaves
> And mounts his black, hard bike.
> Curse-black, hob-nail hard,
> Its saddle flat,
> Sprung,
> And tough as a bog-oak knot.
> Generous trousers strain, compress,
> Their vast blue acres
> Cupping soft,
>
> Pink, drooping mounds.
> Blubber-soft. Piglet-pink. Plush.
>
> Saddle sits coiled, poised, sprung.
> Mounds descend, drooping, pliant, cupped.
>
> Face hangs immobile.
> Eyes like afterthoughts set deep in
> Welts of skull-smothering
> Flesh
> And, rising from the welted mass
> The nose:
> A granite-pocked hillock
> With caves of wire-taut sproutings.
>
> Something stirs. Below the nose,
> Sunk,
> A mouth grins, sensual as slit pork.
> The bike moves off.
> Curse-black.
> Hobnail-hard.
>
> And not a saddle in sight.

19

Philomena, I'm afraid, became impossible to live with on her return from the hospital. Not a day passed but she ordered me out of the house on some pretext or other, usually a product of her fevered female imagination. To my eternal credit I never burdened Francis with any of this, even after the unfortunate incident with the pram. The fact that I bear Philomena no malice concerning this occasion surprises me to this day. Most men, I think, would have cried 'Enough's enough', but I am long-suffering to a fault. I was also motivated by loyalty to my sibling, who would have been devastated had he arrived home to a curt note in place of his youngest living brother.

The circumstances of the above débâcle can be easily related. For whatever reason – maternal incompetence, perhaps? – Philomena's infant cried from one end of the night to the other. I contented myself, selflessly, with sound-proofing my head under the pillow. This, combined with large quantities of cocoa, usually induced sleep without which I can be quite an irritable person. If, however, this method failed I would commence pounding the wall with my fists, but this had the opposite of the desired effect so I made sure that Francis doubled the quantity of cocoa on his weekly shopping list.

During the day the child – a boy, I believe – would habitually sleep off the exertions of the night, while Philomena was usually to be found slumped in front of some appalling televisual representation of life in Australia, often herself asleep. Such was precisely the situation as I was leaving, one afternoon, for the park. I liked to take pen, paper, journal, research notes, flask, light lunch and a spare scarf into the outside world as a break from my more intense poetic activity.

Unable to find an appropriate bag for my various possessions I was struck by the fact that the gap between the child's feet and the end of the pram afforded ample room. I resolved therefore to wheel the child into the park with me. I set off in the best of spirits and, in spite of upsetting some workmen who were laying cement along the footpath and failing to notice an articulated lorry with potentially tragic consequences for my copious notes, we arrived in the park relatively unscathed.

I passed a pleasant couple of hours – days? weeks? – in a state of absolute concentration, broken only by an aggressive looking gentleman's best friend relieving itself against my left leg and a group of youths wishing to retrieve their cricket ball from the pram. Twice. Other than that I could have been in Wordsworth Country, and I tripped home gaily, a happy man.

I had just arrived at the front door when I was met by an hysterical Philomena. Where, she wanted to know, was the baby? I snapped my fingers in irritation. I had often forgotten my flask, my lunch box, or sometimes both, but this time I was without flask, lunch box and my notes. I had left them in the pram. It might be argued that this was because the pram was not normally part of my entourage but Philomena, like many women in times of stress, was not capable of rational discussion. She cut right across my explanation in the rudest way possible and phoned the police.

All was well that ended well. My notes were safe. The child was reunited with its mother well before the park closed for the night. Philomena, as relieved as I was, had a final word to the officer at the door.

'I want this man out of my house,' she shrieked. 'Now.' With that she was gone. The officer tittered through his moustache.

'Tough time for the husband, Sir. Young baby and all that.'

I failed to see what any of this had to do with Francis, but the simple soul obviously meant well so I concurred. He then insisted on showing me pictures of his own children and went on about them in the sentimental way that marks out people of low intelligence. Nothing more was said about Philomena's appalling outburst when I went indoors, but a man has his pride and I seriously considered leaving for a full five minutes afterwards. My suitcase sat on top of a wardrobe and I must have stared at it for some time before transferring my attention to the wardrobe mirror instead.

What I saw before me was a man who had been moulded by the merciless anvil of life into a vessel of integrity, spirit and vision. I squared up to this vision of myself without flinching, nor did my eyes look away but returned my own gaze with studied calm. I imagined myself as the hero of the more challenging class of romantic novel; my steely gaze, firm, jutting jaw and generous, furrowed brow were all attributes of the sort of man women find irresistible, and I resolved to accentuate this image with a pair of cavalry twill trousers and a cravat at the first available opportunity.

Women, or at least the ones I have in mind, are not fools, however, and behind the outward show a hint of gravitas is always welcome. I permitted myself a quiet chuckle. I would certainly not be found wanting in that department. My shock of neo-auburn hair was beguilingly flecked with grey. Behind the calm of my eyes lay the vast deeps of my soul with its dark, murky places, its pools of sunlight and, flashing hither and thither through its fathomless depths, endless varieties of interesting fish.

20

I sat at my desk with some satisfaction shortly afterwards
and tried to write a piece about the afternoon's perambul-
ator incident from the pram's point of view. That I was
unable to do so may have been because the event was too
recent. More likely it was to do with my emotional
involvement. I put it to one side, but without any sense of
failure on my part. Whatever about my sister-in-law's
tantrums, the graph of my professional life was on an
upward curve and I followed madly in its wake.

My parents had been rehoused in an old persons'
compound within walking distance of Heaney's fish shop.
Thanks to a weekly contribution from their state pension
a limited edition of Deep Probings was published at my
own expense.

Like all great works of literature it began its passage
through life alone and unlauded. Initially it was read only
by the select few, but I had reason to believe that my profile

was about to be raised, as witness the following sequence of events.

I am no businessman, but I know enough of the seedy game to understand that a shop will only supply where a demand exists. This, I believe, is known as supply and demand. Prunes, to take but one example. In countries where people don't eat them, shops don't stock them. The onus is then put on the prune farmers of that country to convince the populace that a packet of prunes forms the backbone of the modern shopping list.

As with prunes so, in a more highbrow way, with Deep Probings. The world, I reasoned, was in need of its multi-layered resonances. But it was not yet aware of the fact. With this in mind I decided to visit a selection of bookshops in central London and begin to create exactly that demand. The first bookshop I entered, as luck would have it, featured a popular book signing by 'one of Ireland's finest authors' (*sic*). I won't cheapen this memoir by mentioning the fellow's name, but the priest that every household used to produce has been superceded by the author of bad novels. And this smug young buck was their titular head.

The Bridges of Monaghan County, his latest exercise in word processing, was apparently the story of a passionate, if unconsummated, affair between a pig farmer from Clones and a cello playing prodigy from Minsk. The 'brilliant spin' on the story was that the pig farmer was the woman, which allowed a certain Hollywood actress, once again, to extend her range of accents in a twelve million dollar 'option'.

I passed the row of autograph-hunting sheep in

outraged silence and made my way to one of the few assistants who wasn't drooling over my yarn-spinning compatriot.

'I wish,' I projected, 'to purchase a copy of Deep Probings by artist of the written word Fiachra MacFiach.'

My basso profundo request switched attention away from the preening cretin with the fawning queue.

'Deep Probings?' said the fresh-faced young ignoramus masquerading as a bookmonger. 'Would that be an engineering book?'

'It would not,' I ejaculated. 'It would be, and indeed is, a book of poetry. A poetry book. Filed, no doubt, under Irish but universal in its range and subject matter.'

He looked at me as if he was about to burst into a fit of wails but that was hardly my fault. The use of the term engineering may have been an unintentional slight but a slight it was nonetheless. A woman of more mature years came over and sought to rectify matters.

'You'll find Irish poetry under H for Heaney,' she said, 'but I'm afraid we don't have any MacFiachs in stock at the moment.'

I expressed the hope that she would see to the matter at once, before turning on my heel and marching back to the exit. She accompanied me as I ran the gauntlet of Mr. Pap For The Masses and his fans, held the door with commendable deference and, with a final 'Good day, Mr. MacFiach', went back to join the appalling throng. I walked on, I freely admit, in a state of euphoria. If a lowly shop assistant knew me by name, I reasoned, could fame be far behind?

I don't believe in an external deity, choosing to see God in myself and the odd flower, but some days seem to take on a spiritual dimension as if fated to produce sweet epiphanies. This was obviously one such. No sooner had I left the immediate vicinity of the bookshop than I spotted my old sparring partner, Mr. Scully, striding along on the opposite side of the road. I was naturally curious as to why this enemy of Empire was making his way through the heart of what remained of it. The most obvious reason suggested itself – he had forsaken the cane for the bomb – but my mind was soon put at rest. With a confidence born of previous visits he disappeared into a sado-masochistic emporium of the erotic arts.

What is it about the past that it colours what may well have been traumatic experiences in a rosy glow? The shop in question sparked the memory of my last day at school. Mr. Scully had been in playful mood at the prospect of the long break and was sitting on his desk unravelling some underpant elastic like a kitten with a ball of wool. Sun softened the floorboards and the mood was one of somnambulent ease.

'So tell me, lads,' he said, 'would I have a nickname now by any chance?'

Of course he had a nickname. His nickname was Mad Dog, a sobriquet inherited from his mother. He knew this. He exulted in it. The reason he feigned ignorance? He was simply after the following scenario:

'Your nickname is Mad Dog, Sir.'

'Do you tell me so? Ah sure now isn't that a shocking thing entirely. I must be an awful man so.'

'Ah no, Sir. Hard but fair.'

'Mad dog is it? Well boys oh boys oh boys oh boys oh boys. I must be a right terror and no mistake.'

'Ah no, Sir . . .'

And so on until he was finally convinced of the fundamental soundness of his methods.

On this particular occasion the plan backfired. My fault, I'm afraid. The heat of the sun. The softness of the floor. A bluebottle attempting the impossible flight. And I, the sleepy poet, drowsing in the midst of all, my mind working, working, working. As a mental discipline I had set myself the task of naming all the world's great poets, grouping them in interesting ways to make the task more piquant. Poets whose first language was Ancient Greek, for instance. Poets whose middle name was Clarence. I had just reached American Female Poets Who Committed Suicide when I heard my name in the middle distance.

'Well, MacFiach. What's my nickname?'

The tone was not unkind. It was, as I say, the last day of term. A temporary ceasefire. For this reason, perhaps, I failed to jolt immediately from one world to the other. I vaguely remember deciding to answer the real world question swiftly and return without delay to the world of the limitless imagination.

'Your nickname,' I replied, 'is Sylvia.'

This, as I say, was my final day at school. I was due back the following year but such was the extent of my injuries that it was thought best to keep me on a life support machine.

But now on the streets of Empire, I thought back to this earlier acquaintance and was just about to follow Mr. Scully for a nostalgic reunion when I noticed that the premises immediately adjacent were home to London's most celebrated Irish restaurant, The Great Famine.

deep probings

This in itself was of no great interest to me but I was immediately drawn to a sign on the wall which said Nightly Entertainment. Performers Wanted. Fate? Perhaps. I would normally have run several furlongs from this vision of false jollity, but I had several copies of Deep Probings secreted about my person, and the curious twists and turns of Mr. Scully's life seemed to have led me to exactly that place at exactly that moment. My star appeared to be on the rise.

It must be said in retrospect that the setting was not, perhaps, best suited to the subtle arts. The proprietor, one of my many compatriots willing to usurp historical facts in the mad pursuit of lucre, had established that the world is full of people willing to pay West End prices for the privilege of eating boiled potatoes. I soon found myself in the artists' enclosure with a piano accordionist and a drag artiste referring to himself as the Bootleg Singing Nun. The clientèle included a smattering of preeners from the entertainment world laconically sipping buttermilk.

Any nerves I may have had were banished by the not-unpleasing thought that if the restaurant lived up to its title the same preeners would have been lying across the tables in agonies of malnutrition. Reality, however, soon intruded on this uplifting image. I was summoned to stimulate the jaded palates of the potato eaters. I climbed aboard the rickety stage with a sense of foreboding, justified as it turned out. My arrival coincided with the front table arguing over the bill.

'Desist!' I exclaimed. 'Let the artist speak.'

This was intended as a rallying cry. A summons to lay down their forks and feast, instead, on a plentiful harvest of words. But no. They decided to use what remained of the potato crop as a form of visual criticism. Soon the whole room was at it, gleefully pelting me with a vegetable I have never since liked.

The Bootleg Singing Nun, in a misguided show of solidarity, leapt up on the rickety stage, but this only added to my troubles. A voice began screaming that The Bootleg Singing Nun had ruined her life.

'You _ _ _ _ing abused me, you _ _ _ _,' it roared above the splat of potato against my person and the back wall and, before my brain had articulated a response I was grabbed by the arm and yanked offstage. It was cousin Rosemary.

'Let's get out of here, lover,' she said. 'This is no place for the likes of us.'

In a state of shock outside the restaurant, I was removing yet another Kerr's Pink from my jacket when Mr. Scully emerged from the shop next door. He passed with a look of intense pleasure on his pink and bulbous face. Not noticing us, he danced a jig down Old Compton Street, whacking his generous thigh with a bull whip.

21

My position in London was becoming increasingly untenable. Cousin Rosemary's desire to have a child by an intelligent man was all very well, but I drew the line at being that man myself. She made it clear from the outset, however, that she was accompanying me back to base. When she confided in me that she had begun writing poetry herself, I must admit to an involuntary inward chuckle. Many young girls dabble in verse before settling down, and I made encouraging noises while steering well clear of offering to read the stuff. Lavender-scented pink notepaper does not a poet make and if I have a fault – and I readily admit I am not flawless – it is a complete inability to dissemble. I am nothing if not forthright. I would be forced to confront my cousin with the yawning chasm which separates high art from juvenile tosh. But fortunately I was able to shift the conversation, with utmost delicacy, to myself.

Philomena was in bed on our arrival and Francis was watching the television. An overly familiar face was about to sing the title track from his eponymous recording, 'Yours Truly, Brendan Gilhooley'. Unable to avoid the musical introduction I was at least able to reach the off switch before he burst into song. Rosemary then decided to celebrate our little family get together; she opened a bottle of anis brought back from the continent by Philomena on a honeymoon trip some years previously. Excellent stuff. It loosened Francis up and he began talking wistfully of the lone fellow countrymen staring into their pints at Ward's Irish House without a care in the world. By the time the anis was finished he'd produced a bottle of port which Philomena had been saving up, he slurred, for just such an occasion.

A superb ten-year-old, it was actually seventeen at the time of drinking and we followed it up with a six pack of Beamish purchased by my estimable sister-in-law against an impending visit by her mother, a sachet of add-water-to-taste lager which had been shoved through the door and a home-delivery take-away from Francis' favourite Balti house near his pre-marital address in Luton.

Apparently I used the latter as an excuse to extemporize Where Seventeen Shires Meet, ostensibly the clod Gilhooley's latest single, and I was struggling over Ashby-de-la-Zouch when I fell into a deep sleep.

I awoke some time later with a pounding but a sober head; in full control, therefore, of my estimable faculties. Whatever lingering traces of insobriety remained with me were banished when I returned to my room. Venus entered, Bacchus fled. On the bed, a generous sliver of moon caressing her ever present boots, lay cousin Rosemary, her clothes folded neatly on the bed post. Now I may have seen my mother naked early on in life but the brain is capable of blocking out traumatic events. And what of Widow Bernelle? Who knows? The lights were out.

But here was cousin Rosemary and here was I and here, irrefutably, was the moon. It bathed the sensual scene in shades of muted white. The walls. The bed. The mirror. I caught my reflection and noted that the moon lent a pleasing aspect to my masculine features. The strong jut of my jaw. The proud brow. The gravitas. The depths of my soul. The fish.

Christ, I reflected, spent forty days in the desert. The scene I have lovingly described lasted nothing like forty days, more like five minutes; and when I decided at last to look away from my beautifully lit reflection to my cousin, the muse, that fickle mistress, struck. My hand reached, instinctively, for notebook and pen. The result? Suggestive, perhaps, that my muse was insanely jealous of another woman.

> The moon has been about a bit
> It's Aphrodite's sister
> A naked wench, by moonbeams lit,
> Could any man resist her?
>
> The wench has been about a bit
> The less said there the better
> She'll roast your manhood on her spit
> Consume you if you let her.
>
> The bed has been about a bit
> Its mattress old and fusty
> It's wide enough for two to fit –
> Beware! The springs are rusty.

The finished text, magnificent yet artless though it seems, nonetheless gave me deep pause for thought. What, I found myself fretting, if the springs *were* rusty? I needn't, however, have worried. No sooner had I committed this bawdy, rollicking masterpiece to my journal than I noted, with a poet's keen eye, that the sun was shining and that Rosemary and her clothes had long since left the building.

I would have to watch my step there. Rosemary had passed the sixteen year mark but she was still sexually ambitious. Philomena, too, was becoming increasingly problematic, and things came to a head when she 'completely forgot' – her words – to lay a place for me at the breakfast table. Now I like to think of myself as an easy going sort. It takes a lot to ruffle me. But consider the feelings of a sensitive man at this slight, whether intentional or no. I permitted myself the luxury of a dramatic sigh, that was all. I then sat in Philomena's seat as if nothing had happened and forgave her in my heart.

And yet London, as I say, was becoming a burden. The artist needs space in which to function at his – or, yes, yes, yes, *her* – best. The arrival of my parents' weekly contribution at this juncture seemed almost symbolic in its timing. As previously mentioned, they were presently residing in an old persons' compound within Derry's historic walls. This seemed an ideal place to continue my life's work. Old people are notoriously quiet and, in the odd case where they overstep the mark are much more susceptible than the average person to threats of violence.

I had been visited by the idea of building a perform-ance, based on my life and art, to be offered to some of the more select venues in the English speaking world. The coup de théâtre would be to use the services of an uilleann piper to accentuate the more melancholic segments. I would, I concluded, return to my native land and begin work immediately.

I outlined this plan to Francis and Philomena over breakfast. No sooner had I mentioned the words 'returning', 'native' and 'land' than Philomena's head shot out of the butter dish.

'I'll buy the ticket,' she enthused with such joy on her countenance that I felt I might have seriously misjudged the woman. And true to her word she did so that very morning. I had to question her economic sense in that a return ticket costs no more than a single, but she meant well and economics, to be fair, is not a strong point with most women.

22

So it was that I found myself searching for my parents'
home the following morning. They lived in close proximity
to Heaney's fish shop and, as I had a small matter to thrash
out with the same gentleman, I decided to go there first.
Given the degree of study that would surround my person
in years to come I had decided that my collected letters
would be of invaluable use to scholars of the future. I had
begun keeping copies, but had failed to do so when writing
to Heaney. I wished, accordingly, to make a copy of the
original.

Imagine my horror, then, on discovering that the shop
in question was under new management. Perhaps Heaney
found the world of traffic control more to his taste. Who
knows? But it certainly left me in a difficult spot. I waited
patiently in the queue and outlined my position to the new
proprietor. Mr. Heaney, he informed me sadly, had recently
passed away. Odd, I thought. It doesn't appear to have

deep probings

stopped him writing. I kept this observation to myself and merely commiserated in what must have been a trying time. The death of a fishmonger, I suppose, reminds all other fishmongers of their own mortality.

I then asked what had become of my letter. He professed ignorance of such a letter. I began to detect a shifty look about his eyes. Fishmongers, not unlike the rest of the capitalist breed, are fine tuned to the possibility of making money. A letter from one great artist to another? I could see he was already ordering several tonnes of mullet on the expected proceeds. I put it to him with great respect that he could either give me the letter like a good man or I would be forced to circumnavigate the counter and prise the damned thing from his mercenary grasp.

By this stage a long queue had formed, most of them, it seemed, as ever, pretending to want fish. They could wait, I decided. What was more important – lunch or posterity? My fine friend behind the counter persisted with his ludicrous denial so it was one step onto the hand rail, another into the tray of monkfish and a quick slide, complete with tray, into the freezer.

'Serve away. Don't mind me,' I said as I began searching through the fish carcases, and examining minutely every inch of the back passage. Nothing. He was a wily operator, I had to allow him that. I climbed back over the counter as the police arrived and left under armed escort with only half a kilo of bream – on special offer – to show for my efforts.

I explained my position at the station and the officer on duty looked suitably perturbed. He said nothing, but his look suggested that stealing artists' letters was on the increase and that there was little he could do about it. I was moved to remark that if the local constabulary didn't spend so much time apprehending bombers, polishing their moustaches and indulging in tea breaks, they might begin to make inroads into this most heinous of felonies. The officer at the desk promised to bring the matter up at the highest level but was doubtful it would yield results. It's the culture that needs changing, he said, and that, he concluded, would take some time.

I left the station shortly afterwards, followed a gaggle of ancients round the city walls for several hours and was in due course led unwittingly to my parents' block of flats. I bade them both a curt good morning, requested tea and victuals and immediately set to work.

My first task was to enlist the services of Blind Cearbhúil. He would make me look stunning by contrast. He was home, he was available and by the following afternoon he was parked in the middle of my parents' living room helping me make preparations for an evening of light and shade, of high art and low noise.

Now it may be supposed that an old people's flat would be an ideal place to hold a quiet, uninterrupted rehearsal. Not so. The next door neighbours were listening to the shipping forecast at an unacceptable volume from the outset but that was soon remedied. It was my mother and father who presented the main obstacles to art. Not to mention Cearbhúil himself and the parish priest. If I seem to dwell in detail on what followed it is merely to dissuade other artists from returning to their roots.

There were several problems from the start. The flat was small. I silenced Cearbhúil's first blasting forth on his

deep probings

instrument by requesting that he tune up somewhere else.

'I'm not tuning up,' he replied.

My father, to add to the inconvenience, shuffled about in his wellington boots to no great purpose. Fadharta the Simple placed a couple of stones in the corner of the room and sat glancing at me defiantly. Even my mother was intent on disruption. Her raison d'être had been superceded by the invention of the dishwasher, and this gave her a licence, in her own mind, to wander hither and thither, offering beverages at will. I was busy collating my notes when her head appeared round the door.

'Would yiz like a cup of tea, lads?'

I replied, civilly, that I didn't wish to be interrupted.

'Sorry, son,' she replied. 'Well?'

In order to get the woman out of the room I relented. Two cups of tea. Thank you. Bye now. Blind Cearbhúil sat impassive throughout. Like me, no doubt, wishing the woman would just go away. No such luck.

'What about Cearbhúil?' she said. 'Does he take sugar?'

Now why she was asking *me* I have no idea. I responded that I was an artist. How could she expect *me* to know these things?

'But son,' she whined, 'I can't go making a cup of tea if I don't have all the details. Be fair.'

I looked at her in disbelief.

'Well why not ask someone who does?' I said condescendingly. 'Try phoning his mother.'

'My mother,' said Cearbhúil, 'is dead.'

'Back to square one, son.'

'Well then,' I suggested irritably,' try his Auntie Eileen.'

'Do you have an Auntie Eileen, Cearbhúil?' said my mother. I closed my notebook in disbelief.

'Of course he has an Auntie Eileen. Everyone the length and breadth of this tragic little country of ours has an Auntie Eileen, for God's sake. Even Auntie Eileens have an Auntie Eileen.'

'Fair enough,' said my mother. 'I'll give her a quick buzz so.'

I might have been forgiven for thinking that would be the end of the matter but no; my father chose the exact moment of her departure to shuffle aimlessly in, his wellington boots looking totally incongruous in this cramped urban setting. I was beginning to wish the Brits hadn't bothered burning the old homestead down, especially when my father sat down and proceeded to ogle the television. On it a man was playing a melodeon. I sighed dramatically at this fresh interruption to my tight work schedule.

'What ails you, son?' said my father.

I decided to deal with my grievances point by point.

'Oh, Mr. Uilleann Pipes here for starters,' I snorted. 'How many sugars in his tea has kept us going since we started rehearsing.'

'Sure that's easy enough,' said my father. 'Wouldn't his mammy know?'

'His mother is dead,' I said testily.

'Fair enough. His Auntie Eileen?'

At this point my mother returned.

'There's seventeen Auntie Eileens in the phone book,' she said.

'I only have the one,' said Cearbhúil miserably.

'Is it 47 Kensington Gardens?' said my mother.

'No.'

'12B Cyprus Road?'

'No, no.'

'76 . . .'

'It might be quicker, mother,' I suggested wearily, 'if you asked Cearbhúil where his Auntie Eileen lives.'

'That's exactly what *I* was thinking,' said my father. I examined his large peasant face and doubted it, frankly.

'What?' said my mother. 'You mean ask him where she lives and then match the address with the one in the phone book?'

That, I sighed, was substantially my thesis. My mother was happy again.

'Your Auntie Eileen, Cearbhúil.'

'What about her?'

'Where does she live?'

'Tallahassee.'

My mother's brain was working on this when the parish priest dropped by. He greeted me like the prodigal son.

'We don't see you at mass on Sunday, my child,' he beamed. I bridled at this fresh interruption.

'I've lived several hundred miles away for a number of years,' I said pointedly. 'And besides, I'm a committed atheist to whom the idea of a personal God, a God of wrath and hell fire, an all-knowing God, a God of rage, of ire, a great God almighty who can't be bothered to engage in the simplest form of correspondence with a potential client, is the ultimate absurdity.'

He simpered with false bonhomie.

'Well the Lord save us all,' he said. 'I've heard some excuses in my time but that takes the proverbial biscuit.'

This sort of talk infuriates me and I was happy to abandon my work momentarily on a point of linguistic principle. The family bible stood nearby. I opened it at the relevant section and thrust it at him with mounting fury.

'There's your proverbs,' I said. 'Perhaps you'd be so good as to locate this oft-mentioned biscuit.'

He laughed nervously. Fadharta moved his stones. Mother brightened up.

'Speaking of biscuits, Father,' she said, 'I'm just this minute wetting the tay. Will you have a cup in your hand?'

He closed the book with relief.

'I will so.'

'And do you take sugar, Father?'

'Two spoons, thank you kindly.'

'Fadharta,' said my mother, 'would you ever go to the kitchen like a good boy and bring in the sugar for Father.'

Thirty six year old Fadharta, stupefied by the magnitude of the task, lumbered off excitedly to do her bidding. My mother returned her attention to the priest.

'I only wish,' she pouted, 'that everyone was as easy to deal with.' She dropped her voice conspiratorially. 'We're trying to find out how much sugar Cearbhúil here takes and I'm afraid all the people in the know seem to be gone to a better place one way or the other.'

'Don't talk to me,' said the parish priest. 'We had the same trouble with a one-legged man on the missions.

In the end he got a glass of yak's milk and lumped it.'

'That's all very well, Father,' said my mother, 'but where do you suppose we'd get yak's milk at this time of night?'

I'd had enough. Cearbhúil's disability was going to prove impossible to work with. I gathered up my effects, slipped Fadharta's stones into my bag and made a discreet exit while no-one was looking, so I don't know, to be honest, if Cearbhúil ever got his drink.

23

There are those who would insist that my decision to part company with Cearbhúil showed a lack of compassion on my part. I admit it. Guilty as charged. But I would respectfully suggest that compassion and art don't mix. A fellow poet was castigated for watching an old lady being chased by a rottweiller through a London park. She was eventually impaled on the perimeter railings as she tried to escape. He failed to intervene. If he had, however, how could he possibly have written Lines Composed Upon Watching An Old Lady Being Chased By A Rottweiller And Impaled On The Railings At Finsbury Park? A lacklustre composition, admittedly, but that is hardly the point. Another poet, I believe, went rock climbing with his mother and was inspired by the muse as he guided her up the last few feet. He was presented with the stark choice of grabbing his notebook and biro or maintaining his hold on the rope. He chose as I would have chosen and I'm sure his mother would have supported his decision had she lived, in spite of the fact that the finished product was later consigned to the bin. He couldn't possibly have known that at the time.

At any rate I returned to London. Philomena seemed genuinely stunned.

'You're back,' she cried as I handed her the invoice for the return ticket, her look of dismay no doubt occasioned by the fall-through of my tour. She seemed deeply depressed on my behalf. Perhaps as a result of this, herself and Francis came to the parting of the ways some hours later, which led to Francis leaving the marital home. I don't care to dwell on the following weeks. Suffice it to say they were distressing in the extreme.

Now I am the last person to pontificate, but people should think more carefully before getting married. Had Francis remained single his salary would have been more than adequate for both of us. But there it is. He married in haste, I repented at leisure. His leaving, I'm sad to say, led to a downward spiral which would have broken a lesser man. With the poet's gift of compression, of boiling language down to its essence, the facts can be briefly stated. As soon as Francis had gone Philomena put our flat on the market. I put it to her that I had no wish to move but she was beyond reason at this stage. As a result of her selfish action my life's work was interrupted by an endless stream of estate agents, an odious breed, followed by an equally endless stream of young couples.

I kept my head down and concentrated on my work but Philomena had developed an infuriating habit of showing these wittering galloots round my room. She seemed to be displaying all the signs of mounting hysteria.

'This is the master bedroom,' she'd say, 'and that fine looking specimen with the long jaw is the master.' Much laughter. Or 'Here's Fiachra, the sitting tenant. He comes with the flat.' Much laughter. The endless stream eventually became a trickle and we were left with one couple who insisted on turning up with monotonous regularity and redesigning my room without any consultation on the matter. When lost in the muse I can work in any environment, but I must say I baulked at their notion of painting the room lavender and 'putting the cot by the window.' I said nothing but was determined my personal space wasn't going to be used for storage, new owners or no. I said nothing, but gave vent to my displeasure when asked 'And what exactly do you do, Fiachra?'

'Generally speaking,' I replied, 'I wait for people to leave.'

Philomena's outward cheerfulness, as I say, didn't fool anyone. She was obviously heading for a nervous breakdown. I came to breakfast one morning to find her tut tutting over a copy of the Irish Post. I ate for some time in silence but the tutting continued unabated. She then placed the paper with great deliberation on the table and left the room whistling. I waited till she'd gone, then glanced at the object of her derision and for once, I have to say, it was justified. A book launch, the same morning, by that staple of the poetry lists, the puffed-up amateur. The guest list read like a roll call of our country's most mediocre scribes. No Yeats or Plunkett (J.'M'.) for obvious reasons. Worse. No MacFiach. Philomena came back in.

'Well?' she said.

''Obviously a bureaucratic oversight,' I replied. 'But don't worry. MacFiach will be there.'

I wolfed down what remained of my breakfast, gathered together the tools of my trade and bade farewell to my sister-in-law who, true to her worsening condition, was caterwauling with strident gaiety in the kitchen and wrapping newspaper round plates. The actions of a sane woman? Let me put it this way: I was glad I was going out.

Sometimes, however, we merely swap one set of problems for another. I arrived at the scene of the book launch to be met by a young lady with a clipboard. A steady stream of versifiers filed past as she ticked their names off her list. A rather vacant lot in the main which, given the level of talent, was hardly surprising. Within minutes I stood facing the usherette.

'And you are?' she said.

I was already peeved by the oversight on the invitation front, but that she failed to recognize me was beyond endurance. Do they teach them nothing in school these days?

'Don't be ridiculous,' I said, prising the clipboard from her grasp and ticking a name at random.

Proceedings inside began happily enough. I attacked the buffet with vigour and sped the victuals on their way with several glasses of warm white wine. While doing so I gave my rivals the once over. None, of course, withstood the intense scrutiny of my piercing intellect. Pygmies! Minnows! Nitwits! I was on the verge of declaiming this point with Ciceronian vim when a woman in a three-piece suit joined me by the wine. I noted with interest that she was cultivating the left side of a moustache. The inference was hard to miss.

'Hello, Miss Plunkett,' I said.

An apposite guess. She winked at me in a masculine sort of way.

'Hello yourself.'

I launched into a vigorous defence of her great uncle and remarked that I was planning a biography when my own genius was recognized. I then went on to give her a detailed account of my life-in-progress. This riveting discourse was interrupted, I'm sorry to say, by the efforts of an earnest looking poseur of inflated reputation trying to convince the young woman on the door that he couldn't possibly be there already as here he was, arriving. This altercation was distasteful in the extreme and it is to the credit of the management that he was physically ejected.

It did, however, have the negative effect of interrupting my flow and Miss Plunkett took this as a cue to trumpet her own accomplishments. In retrospect it was just as well.

'Oh,' she said, rubbing quiche from her facial growth, 'I don't go in for this poetry lark at all myself. I'm here for the wine.'

I felt myself cooling towards the woman.

'And what exactly do you do?' I enquired.

'I'm a senior civil servant as it happens,' she replied.

She was about to regale me with the intimate details of her tedious profession but I was rescued from this depressing vista by the commencement of speeches from the stage. Reflecting on how far the Plunkett gene had plummeted, not to mention how low the civil service now set its sights, I bade her good day, purloined a couple of glasses of tepid Liebfraumilch and moved closer to the forthcoming action.

Proceedings were opened by an Australian 'poet' of generous girth who spoke, at interminable length, about himself. I switched off, to be frank. 'Australian' and 'poet' fit together, I mused, like 'German' and 'wine'. I returned to the Liebfraumilch table and, reflecting that 'Waltzing Matilda' had a lilting melody, began humming it involuntarily. I was shushed by several people in the immediate vicinity and have to admit I took their point. The tune is as bland as the lyric.

When I returned to my place at the front our Antipodean friend had been replaced by the guest speaker. And the guest speaker turned out to be none other than the model used by the late Seamus Heaney for his publicity shots. If he had been introduced as such then fair enough. But this appalling chancer was masquerading as the man himself. I downed both glasses in mounting fury.

'Heaney' (*sic*) was just getting into his stride when I interjected to startling effect.

'You, Sir,' I announced, 'are an impostor. A charlatan. The worst sort of con man.'

The room fell silent, stunned by my powerful rhetoric. 'If we must have Heaney,' I continued, 'then let us have the real Heaney and not this sop to the market place; this glamorous front.'

'I *am* the real Heaney,' said 'Heaney'.

I was ready for this.

'Aha!' I said, suppressing an almost physical attack of glee. 'In that case you'll have the answer to the following three questions at your fingertips. What is the present price of prawns?' Silence. 'When is the high season for rock salmon?' Silence. 'How many whelks, on average, in a tub?' The embattled mountebank looked visibly shaken. 'See? *Quod erat demonstrandum.* I rest my case.'

Knowing that my point had been proven with force I withdrew with dignity. I am not a vindictive man. 'Heaney' had been unmasked. He would have to face the consequences. My work was done. I felt the warm glow of admiration on my back as I marched past my pseudo peers and out into the early afternoon sun.

I wandered around for a while before getting my bearings and eventually arrived home around teatime. I noticed a skip outside the flat and, sitting on top of it, my suitcase. On closer examination it proved to have been packed. Curious, I thought, but it was that sort of day. I retrieved it, struggled over the key-hole for a time, and let myself in.

If the suitcase on the skip incident was odd, then locating a cot in my newly painted bedroom was puzzling in the extreme, especially as it contained a sleeping child. I was baffled but determined; I wasn't sharing my room with anyone. But I decided to check the lie of the land first. No sense in getting upset without having the full facts at my disposal. I opened the door to the dining room and there sat the Lavenders, as I called them, enjoying their evening meal. They seemed somewhat surprised to see me, to be honest. Perhaps they thought book launches went on all night. I decided to put them at their ease.

'No tea for me thanks,' I said. 'I'm up to here with quiche.'

I pulled a chair up and gave them a scene by scene

deep probings

account of the unfolding drama and my central role in it, guffawing loudly when I came to the bit about the fish.

'The thing is,' I roared, thumping the table with relish, 'I didn't know the answers myself. The fool could have lied.'

I then made a couple of disparaging comments about Liebfraumilch, excused myself and went for a long walk to relieve my aching head. When I returned a 'Do Not Disturb' sign hung on the front door, the locks had been changed and my suitcase had been relocated, still neatly packed, on top of the skip. As Rosemary, apparently, had left no forwarding address – an oversight which was typical of the woman – I was temporarily homeless.

I spent the evening contemplating what to do. I could hardly return to my parents house at such short notice. Cearbhúil, no doubt, would still be sitting there waiting to start rehearsals. I was also unwilling to retrace my steps to Dublin. Cousin Rosemary would, I felt sure, arrange to be there coincidentally, and I had begun to have grave doubts about my ability not to father her child. Falling asleep had come to my rescue on one notable occasion but Morpheus might not always be so obliging in his timing. Not surprisingly, the following extract from my journal, which I don't remember writing, gave me serious pause for thought on this subject.

> I fell victim to the most appalling nightmare which I propose to outline in detail as an insight into the troubled psyche of the creative artist. I am offered a lecture tour of the American Mid West as a great Irish artist. The contract stipulates that I wear faded tweeds with leather arm patches and am constantly inebriated for purposes of authenticity. I honour the

contract in letter and spirit, returning to civilization some months later with no recollection whatsoever of my trip, such has my degree of intoxication been throughout. When I finally sober up I find myself in a strange bed. A well-built woman with a purple rinse lies sleeping ominously beside me. Her passport sits next to her tooth mug. I open it with trembling hands. One of the Minnesota Mermans as was, she is now Mrs. Ethel MacFiach. I note a pile of Mid Western press cuttings.

'Irish Poet Blazes Love Trail Across States.'

'Irish Poet Weds Hooker In Reno Parking Lot.'

'Irish Poet Romances Post Box.'

I conclude that my resistance to alcohol has its limits and am about to panic when a brace of large pre-teens with crewcuts and raisin eyes lumber in.

'Hi, Mom,' they say. 'Hi, Dad.'

DAD?! I leap out of bed noting, too late, that I'm wearing only my scarf.

A dream, assuredly, but a warning too. Poets in their cups are noted for waking up with different people, many of them women, and the higher the number the greater the possibility that one of them will be called Ethel, or, to return to my original thesis, Rosemary.

For this reason, a return trip to Dublin was out and I was pondering my other options – there weren't any – when the problem was solved on my behalf. I was ambling along a side street in a dejected fashion when two men with stockinged heads sprinted round the corner. They were about to dash past when the one in front stopped suddenly.

'Jayzus! Fiachra!' he said. 'I haven't seen you in years. How the hell are you?'

I replied that I was fine as far as it went and was about to ask if he could put me up for a while, whoever he

deep probings

was. But no! He started reminiscing about the old days and how they all had great hopes for my future and wasn't it terrible what the Brits did to the house while his friend frisked about beside him in an agitated manner.

'Well anyway,' he concluded, 'can't stand round here chatting all day. Things to do. Places to be.'

At that moment a police siren started up and with a final 'Here! Hold this!' he was off. As the police car turned the corner I found myself holding an old acquaintance's pistol, which guaranteed a roof over my head for some time to come.

If I had known anything about the conditions of my tenancy I might have thought twice about accepting the weapon in the first place. I refused to 'grass', as they put it, on my 'mates', for the simple reason that I didn't know who they were. The chatty one did a good impression of my brother Ferdia, but men who wear stockings over their heads usually do so for purposes of anonymity and I felt I had to respect their right to privacy. My principled stand led to an eventful couple of days with several interrogating officers which brought me back, not without nostalgia, to my years with Mr. Scully. I didn't even have to draw a map of Ireland for this lot. I still remember clearly the three concurrent thoughts that preceded my first black-out.

That the pleasure they took in their work was almost infectious.

That a state of temporary homelessness approaches the idyllic when measured against the alternative.

That the ability to think three different thoughts simultaneously is perhaps at its most acute when a heavily moustachioed detective is sitting on your face.

I spent some considerable time on remand awaiting trial and propose to gloss over this period. Why? I failed, frustratingly, to get one iota of writing done. I was understandably livid and have since tried to block the experience from my mind. I was forced to share my quarters, it pains me to report, with a low type whose background was in the rarefied world of the fun fair. If we had both been writers we could no doubt have come to some arrangement, but I felt my cell mate had within him the capacity for physical unpleasantness and was best given as wide a berth as our cramped conditions could afford. I also felt, instinctively, that divulging my profession might not work to my advantage. I kept a wary eye on him most of the time and, after a few attempts to draw me out he left me to my own devices.

I had some writing materials hidden away and once or twice attempted a quick verse when he dozed off but, although I concealed the notebook within a pornographic magazine or Stevedore Quarterly in case he woke up suddenly, the conditions were hardly ripe for creativity.

24

Intellectually, then, a barren time. Stevedore Quarterly is not without merit – it is, for instance, well bound, and a series of colour prints of naked women in building site helmets suggest that rugged, outdoor work is not the male preserve of popular myth – but I pined for a different sort of stimulation. And this came, when it did, from an unlikely quarter. A group of Irish prisoners soon got wind of my presence and it transpired that I enjoyed something of a cult status with same. I found this immensely gratifying. I seemed to remember some of them from school, mainly friends of Ferdia, and they began to make quite a fuss over me.

There's nothing quite like a period of incarceration to make an otherwise below average intellect yearn for culture, and it wasn't long before my presence acted as the catalyst for a Celtic Studies group which soon attracted sufficient numbers to warrant official recognition and a cell of its own. The scope, initially, was broad in the extreme and took the form of a general discussion overlooked by a couple of burly, moustachioed warders, both of whom dropped out of active involvement within minutes and took to wandering about in the corridor engaging in mindless prattle.

After a couple of months, however, a curious change began to take place. I had been treated with deference so far and it was now being suggested that I give a poetic master-class, concentrating on my own work, with which some of the more enlightened were no doubt already familiar. Naturally I was pleased to do so and discovered, in this collection of social outcasts, a responsive audience which pounced with delight on my every metaphor.

This, then, became our regular diet. A brief discussion, followed by a recital, always given by myself. The odd interruption was quickly dealt with. On one occasion, as I was about to begin, my cell mate drifted in, intrigued perhaps by the sustained burst of applause which greeted my opening salvo. I was frozen to the spot. This was the last thing I wanted.

My restless audience, seeming to sense this, turned and stared at him in silence until, cowed into submission he wandered, head bowed, back whence he came. I then returned to my reading with renewed vigour, my sonorous voice and dramatic gestures provoking involuntary and sustained applause in the unlikeliest places as the warders, unable to deal with the spiritual intensity of the experience, remained outside debating the simplicities of their own small souls and world.

Great poetry reveals itself slowly and it's hardly

surprising that the group was keen to hear my work at every available opportunity. Perhaps because prison life accentuates the patriarchal they developed a particular fondness for the image of my father digging and put it to the warders that the physical presence of a small amount of wet, brown clay would immeasurably further appreciation of the poem. The warders chuckled and stood on the balls of their feet.

'You find it, Pat, you can have it.'

Find it, I have to say with undisguised admiration, they did. And, in addition, from I knew not where, a spade. The gnarled tree, it was pointed out, they could live without. So it was that Lines for Seamus Heaney became the focal point of our by now thrice-weekly meetings, and each reference to wet, brown clay was met by vigorous and sustained applause of such duration that I felt that here, at last, I had found my audience. I was often prevailed upon to render the poem in question, to an increasingly rapturous response and, as if in physical reflection of the concerns of my art, the volume of wet, brown clay began to increase. One of the warders, at the end of a particular session, quipped merrily that you never find an Irishman far from his shovel, but the leader of our group snapped that this was a racist remark and the warder was forced to retract his comment.

I was naturally delighted at the response to my work but was moved to point out that we might have sufficient in the way of wet, brown clay to illustrate the poem's main image. (It was becoming increasingly difficult to find space for seats.) I was reassured by the explanation that the volume of clay reflected, in physical form, the growing understanding of the work in question. And the seats were shortly to become redundant anyway.

A most odd occurrence. I had begun yet another rendition of our favourite piece when I became aware that the applause, though genuine and prolonged as always, seemed more muted on this particular occasion. I read it three times that evening and each time the response was less and less voluminous.

'One more time, Fiachra,' said the group leader and, when I reached the line about clay it was greeted by a solitary clap. Perhaps, I felt, I had peaked with that particular work. I am always wary of overdoing things. Looking at my audience I noticed that the seats were bare. The wet, brown clay was piled neatly to one side. Between the first and second row the group leader waved farewell and disappeared down a hole which, it transpired, they had been digging for some time.

The governor at first tried to hold me responsible but it soon became apparent that I was an artist of the highest integrity and that culpability lay with a hard core of troublemakers intent on disrupting the cultural betterment of others. The explanation for the hole was that it formed the entrance to a tunnel through which the Celtic Studies group had vacated the premises. I begged leave to doubt that they would find an educational facility to match it on the outside and that the brighter ones would be back.

The warders seemed to have forgotten granting permission for the clay – I jogged their memories, naturally – and the governor asked me to accompany them down the tunnel in case I had anything else of value to contribute. What we discovered was a narrow gap, scarcely big enough to walk two abreast, which led to a taxi rank half a mile from the main gate. The tunnel was fully lit and tastefully decorated in beige wallpaper. It contained, at its centre, an extended section with multi-channel television set, mini bar and a comfortable if slightly shop-soiled three-piece suite. The warders seemed quite upset by the whole business and embarked on a damage limitation exercise for the benefit of the media, which piled in from the taxi rank end. There was, they said, at least no aspidistra. I was happy to enlighten them on this point. The aspidistra, I explained, is a symbol of domestic harmony for the English lower middle classes. The closest Irish equivalent would be a statue of the Blessed Virgin Mary, one of which sat here in pride of place on the mantelpiece, directly under the three flying popes.

The governor was genuinely grateful for my co-operation but felt that it would set a bad precedent if he rewarded me with a spell in solitary confinement. I was back where I started. Common incarceration. The daily grind. The mind-numbing passage of days. Stevedore Quarterly. The spring edition had just been published but this was of little interest to me. Nor for that matter was the summer one that followed, nor the autumn or winter. They merely marked the inexorable march of time, the relentless ticking of the clock which hastens us all to our end whether we be king or commoner, poet or peasant, or, for that matter, editor of Stevedore Quarterly.

25

I was rescued from inertia, oddly enough, by a surprise visit
from the Clooney twins, Joel and Ethan. I have failed, before
now, to mention their curious habit of finishing each other's
sentences. What surprised me more on the occasion of their
visit, however, was, not the way they said it, but what they had
to say. While I was honing my art in obscurity they, it
transpired, had been working their way up in the world of
cinema. I wasn't really listening, my views on cinema being
well documented, but they appeared to be meandering
towards some sort of point. Their most recent film – Nine
Hundred and Eighty Six Years A-Growing: The Life and
Times of Methuselah – had been, apparently, a palpable hit.

But what, I asked, had that to do with me?

I freely admit I was delighted – but not surprised –
by what they had to propose. They wished, said Ethan, to
use my life, elaborated Joel, as the subject of a film,
concluded his brother. The development of my genius

would supply the narrative thrust. They had followed my progress with fascination and had been given background detail by a host of interviewees. My parents. Philomena. Mr. Scully. Bridie's father. They had even traced Assumpta the Ass to a field in Athenry. And yet I still remained to be convinced that they were in earnest.

I had been captured on film once before and it had been a salutary experience. My journal (Volume XLIV) captures this episode with limpid, stylish prose.

'Philomena', it begins, 'is in many ways a fine woman and I am happy to put my dirty clothes at her disposal. My scarf, however, is sacrosanct. I took it to the local launderette this afternoon and, as always, brought pen and notebook with me. Although locked in concentration my creative juices failed to flow. I sat impassive, pen poised above paper, while my scarf struggled ineffectually with the tumble drier. (This image of my scarf as reluctant prisoner is typical of my attention to poetic detail.) I returned home some time later and was naturally startled to find the scene replayed on a popular television programme.

'Have you seen this man?' the presenter was asking and yes, there I was, pen poised, face set in an attitude of supreme concentration. Behind me a man with a knife was relieving the launderette's proprietor of his takings in a most aggressive manner, but such was my attention to the absent muse that I noticed nothing. This, of course, was the raison d'être of the piece: to alert artists to the need for total concentration.'

I was about to mention this incident, and the fact that I came away without my scarf, when the twins broached it themselves. They had seen it. They felt exactly as I did. So strongly did they feel about it, indeed, that a re-enacted version, entitled Writer's Block, had been shot by themselves as a short feature and had been shown to great acclaim out of competition, out of festival, out of season, at Cannes.

I was impressed by their efforts so far and finally decided to give them full access to my notebooks when they showed me a transcript of the opening scene of their proposed script. It was me to the life. I transpose it with due humility.

EXT. DAY. FIELD AT BACK OF COW SHED.

FIACHRA AS BOY STANDS IN FIELD IN PAIR OF WELLINGTON BOOTS. TWO BOYS CHECK CAMERA ANGLES AND LIGHTING.

FIRST BOY
Hold it right there, Fiachra . . .

SECOND BOY
We're just off to save up . . .

FIRST BOY
For a box camera.

TWO BOYS WALK OFF. FIACHRA HOLDS POSE.

TITLES

DARKNESS FALLS. FIACHRA STILL THERE.
FADE.

Stunningly cinematic, but I had one final question, simply to put my mind at rest. Was this to be another

Irishman-wrongly-imprisoned blockbuster? Nothing of the sort, they responded. They were both convinced that I was guilty. Which brings me to another curious point about this decidedly odd pair. Their assumption that I had some involvement with proscribed organisations can hardly be said to enter the realm of the comic. And yet both parties were visited by uncontrollable fits of mirth on this and other occasions, usually when I was in full flow. Far from wishing to ridicule a man of my exalted stature, however, it transpired that they suffered from an incurable medical condition: gelastic seizures, or the inability to refrain from laughing.

This unfortunate affliction hindered our progress somewhat, and I was moved to remark, with dry and pithy wit, that if the medical profession spent less time rushing round hospitals interfering with artists' creativity, and concentrated on their work, they could rid the world of such pernicious ills twice over. I was about to expand on my thesis but was drowned out by fits of weeping and thigh slapping which are, apparently, regular symptoms of this vexatious scourge.

On the other hand, knowing that my life was to be the subject of a serious reappraisal was a source of great comfort to me throughout the period of my imprisonment. My inability to write rankled, but I was visited on a weekly basis by the twins and was able, in the brief moments when their affliction abated, to unburden myself of some of my theories and clarify points in the journals. I also basked in their obvious admiration at my ability to affect the lives of all I touched, in the pursuit of one small but glowing masterpiece.

'A rose,' said Joel,

'On the dung-hill of life,' concluded his brother.

Beautifully put, I thought at the time, and ideal for the foreword of my forthcoming memoir. I resolved to write the phrase down as soon as I was free.

26

I was also to make another, more far-reaching, resolution. On their final visit the brothers gave me a small book bearing the Faber and Faber imprint. My initial response was one of profound shock. It was none other than the maiden slim volume of cousin Rosemary – The Seduction and Other Poems. I couldn't believe it. As soon as her brothers had left I shot to the back cover.

> 'Reflects a poet's sensibility. Taut and honed to the whim of word and image.'
>> Seamus Heaney (London Review of Books)

> 'Word and image juxtaposed in a taut, honed reflection of poetic sensibility.'
>> Seamus Heaney (Times Literary Supplement)

I was stunned. Cousin Rosemary: a poet. But as to being taut and honed, I rather doubted it, somehow. Heaney, of course, could be relied upon in matters of fish as long as you double checked your change, but poetry is a different matter. I opened the book.

'To My Muse – F.' it said.

Good God, I thought. Who was F? I glanced quickly at the titles.

'Nun.'

'The Great Famine.'

'Joseph 'Mary' Plunkett.'

'Algebra.'

A blank page, the latter. I turned frantically to the title poem and reprint the piece here in full to save people the bother of buying the book.

THE SEDUCTION

I had it all. The soft white flesh
The curving inner thighs
The moon was on my side
The night
The element of surprise.
My living sculpture lay in wait
To trap his burning eyes.

I rearranged my subtle limbs
The bed and I both bare
I lay in wait and heard his foot
Upon a creaking stair
Then I lay here
In silence
And he stood
Silent
There.

He stood
Transfixed and rooted
For hours in a daze
Behind me
cold and silent

In moon-enchanted ways
The mirror on the wall returned
His passionate
Longing
Gaze.

Not without promise, undoubtedly, but hardly meriting the hyperbole on the back cover. It was ever thus: mere talent is rewarded with the baubles and trinkets of the market-place while genius – brain-disturbing, mould-breaking genius – languishes on remand. Besides, it was a wardrobe mirror.

And yet. And yet. While it is certainly true that she was a mere girl, and the fawning reviews undoubtedly betray a patronizing tone on closer inspection, she was not, as I say, without promise. Under my tutelage she might even amount to something, especially if she could be encouraged to avoid the gaudy circus of inflated, publicity-seeking egos parading themselves as poets in the modern world. It was certainly worth thinking about.

I looked again at the dedication.

'To my muse, F.'

My God! I, Fiachra F. MacFiach. It was I!

I readily admit that this new perspective began to have a profound effect on me. Perhaps I'd been wrong. Perhaps it was possible to pursue a wild romance and still be a great poet. I thought of William Wordsworth and Dorothy. Of . . . well, that was enough to be going on with. I began to visualize the scene. Cousin Rosemary rapt with attention as I read from my journal, guiding her ineluctably in the direction of minor greatness. Long walks by the river. Passionate couplings enveloped in a double-length scarf. Rosemary waiting on tables to bring in the necessary finance to propagate my work, and happily typing up my manuscripts in the odd lull.

Being a woman she would probably want children. Fine.

'But don't,' I found myself admonishing, 'expect MacFiach to weigh in.'

An affectionate pat on the head once a fortnight? Why ever not. The day-to-day mundanities? Sorry, but no. Busy busy busy. Writer at work.

This, of course, is to look on the positive side. What, then, of the negative aspect? What if, as so often happens when poets marry, she committed suicide? This was not, on mature reflection, an entirely negative prospect. It would boost sales of both our books and no doubt spur me on to a fine study of bereavement. No. My mind was made up. Rosemary was the woman for me. I would inform her of my plans in person at the next available opportunity.

And that happy occasion, I am pleased to report, was soon to arrive. After some two years in detention my case was heard and my defence was able to produce a witness who had seen the whole sorry business. The judge eyed her beadily as she took the stand.

'I demand to know this woman's sexual history,' he said.

'With all due respect, my Lord,' said my defence, 'the witness is not in the dock.'

'I'll be the judge of that,' said the judge. 'I am, after all, the judge. What were you wearing at the time?'

'I fail to see what this has to do with the proceedings against my client,' protested my defence.

deep probings

'It may have nothing, it may have everything. Well?'

The judge was eventually prevailed upon to deal with my alleged crime but seemed baffled when my defence came to the fact that I may have known one of the men.

'He may have been my client's brother, your honour,' she said.

'May have been?' said the learned judge. 'Surely your client might be expected to recognize his own brother.'

'He has sixteen brothers, my Lord.'

'Ah.'

'Besides, the men in question were wearing stockings at the time.'

'Stockings? What? Women's stockings?' He brightened up and peered at me. 'Is there a history of this sort of activity in your family, young man?' I was about to demur when he looked at his notes. 'MacFiach,' he said. 'MacFiach. Sweet Alis MacFiach. Nothing to do with you, I suppose?'

'My paternal grand-uncle,' I replied.

'Do you tell me so?' He mellowed slowly and his grizzled face took on a softer, more boyish look. 'D'you know I never missed one of his performances when I was studying for the bar. The gay nineties we used to call them. And so they were. So,' he sighed, 'they were.' He sat up. 'What sort of stockings?'

'One was black silk, the other more flesh coloured. Most likely nylon. Fifteen denier I would think although I didn't get that close a look.'

He peered at me over his glasses.

'You seem to know a lot about such matters, young man,' he said.

'I am an artist, sir,' I replied. 'I make it my business to know.'

'You're a credit to your uncle,' he replied, beaming. 'Excellent,' he continued. 'So we've established that you were set upon by two one-legged transvestites, one of whom may have been your brother. That much is clear.'

The case dragged on for some weeks. The learned judge, in his summing up, said that too often women, by their code of dress and brazen conduct, by their misplaced desire for equality and the fact that the words ideal and home seldom feature together in the feminist lexicon – he paused here until his laughter had died down – were simply asking for it. And it appeared that this brazen use of a come hither style of dress was spreading, disturbingly, to the criminal classes. Whatever our personal views on the matter, he concluded, the law was the law and must be seen to be applied in an even handed way regardless of codes of dress. I was, in a word, given two years for receiving stolen property.

Two years. That meant that I had precisely twenty minutes left to serve. Just sufficient time to gather together my effects, while my cell mate of those wasted days swung his feet morosely on the top bunk. As I was leaving he looked sheepishly at me and asked if it was true I was a poet. With a moustachioed guard at the door, and further protected by the fact that we would never meet again – I don't make a habit of consorting with criminals – I answered that yes, I was a poet, a great poet, and that I was proud to declare the fact before the whole world if necessary. He extended a large tattooed hand.

'I like poetry,' he said. 'It's been a privilege to know you.'

27

Aware that my brother and sister-in law had failed in their familial reponsibilities, Joel and Ethan met me at the prison gate. They had arranged a place for me to stay and when I saw it I was, as I recall, deeply touched. A one-bedroom flat in one of London's less seedy districts, it had been decorated in my honour. Pictures of me lined the walls. Blown up reproductions of my verse resided in glass cases. In pride of place on the shoe rack sat a spawn-flecked pair of child's galoshes (circa 1970). A full length mirror greeted me as I entered the bedroom, where my best striped pyjamas lay draped over a chair, and I admired, in passing, the mature artist I had become.

Other than that the rooms were reassuringly spartan. A cooker. A bed. Table and chairs. Several full length mirrors scattered about the place. The one odd feature was that two people, a man and a boy, appeared to be in residence already. As we entered they were wandering about with pen and notebook in hand, extremely severe of countenance, both wearing wellington boots. We were not introduced and I was so taken with the general decor that the moment passed.

Joel and Ethan gave me their telephone number and a set of keys and left. The two residents stayed where they were. As I say the moment had passed so I decided it might be best to ignore them. Besides, I had been too long away from my art and so, not wishing to waste time in banter, I sat at the kitchen table with great anticipation and set to work.

At least I would have set to work, but I had the odd sensation that the above-mentioned were examining me closely. They procured chairs themselves and sat down at the same table. I stared at the blank page of my notebook and tried to concentrate but it was impossible. I looked up suddenly. They looked away. I was right. For reasons best known to themselves I exerted an enigmatic hold over them. All very flattering, I felt, but what if it carried on indefinitely? I resolved to phone Joel and Ethan on the subject.

This, of course, was more difficult than simply picking up the phone and dialling a number. People, after all, are notorious for listening in on private conversations, especially when conducted in the same room. They would be bound to notice we were discussing them. So I would have to wait until I was on my own, but they seemed content to sit where I was sitting and do what I was doing.

I sat. I couldn't write. They sat. They couldn't write. The boy raised his pen and glared at me.

'This is my spade,' he said. 'I'll dig with it.'

The man did likewise.

'I am an artist,' he declaimed. 'I demand sustenance in return for which I will entertain you with verses to delight the mind.'

This went on for some time. Hours? Weeks? Eventually I decided to break the deadlock and go to bed. I went to the lavatory, brushed my teeth, entered the master bedroom, shut the door, disrobed, put my pyjamas on and got into bed. I lay still. The lavatory flushed twice in quick succession. I heard two sets of teeth being brushed. A short silence. Then the door opened and my persecutors got into bed on either side of me, both wearing identical striped pyjamas. Exactly the same as mine, in fact. I had never, to my almost certain knowledge, been in a similar situation and could find no precedent in any work of literature I had read, whatever the language of origin. It was difficult, therefore, to know how to respond. I decided, in the end, to get some sleep and attempt to resolve the matter on the morrow.

It was a comfortable bed after my prison experience but I slept badly in spite of this. I tossed, they turned, and vice versa. It was difficult developing any sort of coherent rhythm, especially after the elder of the two, his black, intense eyes piercing mine, murmured 'Your name is Sylvia.'

I was quite relieved when morning came and enabled me to put an end to the proceedings. I sat up. They took this as their cue to rise. I abluted. They abluted. We dressed. I held back slightly, allowing them to finish before me. I thought they might slow up themselves, but they seemed to know what they were doing without my help.

They finished dressing, loaded two pans up with the makings of Ulster fries, took possession of their notebooks and pencils and, with looks of preoccupation on both their faces, left the flat. As they did so the boy returned my glower with a glower of his own.

I was astonished and relieved at once and phoned my cousins, as soon as they had closed the door, for an explanation.

'Didn't we tell you?' they said.

'That's Fiachra Junior'

'and Fiachra Senior.'

'They're'

'the male'

'leads.'

I slammed the phone down in outrage. I had just, against all the tenets of morality, integrity and plain common sense, slept with a couple of actors.

28

Perhaps, in the end though, it would all be worth it. I was aware that cinema, although a minor art form, was capable of alerting the world to the presence of a greater one, and the twins had a duty to perform. But the impending film made concentration difficult. I began to look forward to its release and the resultant increase in sales of my work; the queues round the block at my book signings; the pleasure of seeking out anonymity rather than having it thrust upon me; the feeling that posterity was going to honour me while I was still young enough to enjoy it. I had also chosen the premiere as the ideal backdrop for my forthcoming proposition to cousin Rosemary. The anticipation of her delight made the delay more than worthwhile.

I had one further reading before being summoned to the premiere and if I describe it in some detail I do so merely to illustrate the contrast with my prison experience, a golden age in comparison. Here are the bald facts. A folk music artist named Dillon – no Christian name if you please – was performing a concert in an intimate setting in north London. My cousins had met the man before and had mentioned me to him in glowing terms. The consequence was that I was cordially invited to expand my audience by giving one of my celebrated readings at this same concert. Disarmed, as I say, by the twins' humility and lulled by the reference to my other celebrated readings I submitted graciously to their request. Someone had to fill the blessed hall.

It was only afterwards that the implications of my promise filtered through. I made some inquiries into the Dillon character's work and realised that I was acquainted with his songs. They blared out so relentlessly from every underground station around London you'd be forgiven for thinking there was more than one of him. He was employed to sing them in an effort, I imagine, to make people walk faster, and the notion that he would fill a hall with people actually wanting to sit still was, frankly, ludicrous. It suggests an all too common case of arrogance outstripping talent.

On the other hand, if he was foolish enough to hire a hall without bothering to publicise the event, I might as well benefit. I decided, for that reason, to publicise it myself. A few sheets of A4 attached to trees in the local park would alert a wide cross section of the local populace so I set about the task with relish. I agonized, naturally, over the detail. The performance was, after all, Dillon's idea. Perhaps I should reflect this in the billing. But 'Dillon'? I wrote it at the top of a sheet of paper and quite honestly it didn't work. Some people can get away with only one name. Christ, for instance. 'Do you believe that Christ died for your sins?' No need here for 'Which Christ did you have in mind?' Dillon, however, is less specific. 'I hear Dillon is performing unpublicised at a small venue in north London.' This is hardly likely to set the pulse racing. MacFiach, on the other hand, has a certain ring to it. 'Have you read the latest MacFiach?'

My decision was made.

MACFIACH
(ARTIST OF THE SPOKEN WORD)

PLUS SUPPORT

I forgot to bring sellotape into the park, but the gods were smiling. Someone had recently put a pitiful lost dog notice up in several places and had been more than generous with the blue tack. It was the work of minutes to remove these – the dog, I felt sure, must have had his reasons – and replace them with my own. And I'm delighted to report that they produced the desired effect. The venue in question was packed.

I made several fruitless attempts to speak with the Dillon character before curtain up but he was permanently surrounded by others. Creditors? I had no way of knowing but was willing to bet it was his first full house. I had no burning desire to speak to the man. I merely wished to establish which of us was to open the proceedings, but the first sour note of the evening was struck when I was called to start the show without any proper consultation. This insult was compounded by the fact that Dillon must have been a party to it. Arrogance stroke talent? Point proven, I fancy.

I don't wish to dwell on my performance. Suffice it to say that the audience comprised thousands of paying customers, and whatever else they were there for, cultural enlightenment was obviously not on the list. I have since established beyond reasonable doubt that people who drink strong ale out of plastic glasses are rarely in pursuit of intellectual stimulation. This particular mob also appeared to find, in the same glass, an acceptable substitute for the boiled potato. As the first wave flew past I made my excuses and left.

The rather pallid looking 'main act' (*sic*) was waiting in the wings. He mumbled something incomprehensible which didn't augur well for his chances with the mob. And yet I felt a certain sympathy. If they treated a bona fide genius to a hail of plastic what would happen to a man awkwardly plying his trade with a child's guitar?

'I wouldn't bother if I were you,' I said in a kindly, avuncular sort of way. 'They're a pack of animals out there.'

He mumbled something else I failed to catch and marched off to meet his doom, blatantly ignoring my sound advice. I had seen old newsreel footage of young men going over the top in the Great War and had no desire to be reminded of it. I had done my best to alert him to his fate; he had failed to take my advice. So be it. The roar that greeted his arrival on stage was frightening in its intensity and was, without doubt, far worse than my reception. The crowd, I felt, was after blood. I left by the back door and have not seen or heard of him since.

29

I was well on the way to recovery from this experience when I was contacted again by my cousins with an official invitation to the charity premiere of The Genius – an apposite title – in their native city. A car to the airport, chartered flight to Dublin, open top bus, that sort of thing. And, though unostentatious to a fault, I decided there might be a poem in it. Besides, the prospect of waving to the masses from a great height seemed, as I caught sight of my profile in a strategically placed mirror, entirely appropriate.

Feeling distinctly peckish as I awaited the arrival of the car I placed some victuals on the stove, checked my profile in the mirror again and looked out the window. What appeared to be a stretch Volkswagen had pulled up outside and a man in a peaked cap was getting out. I made sure I had everything, donned my best scarf and . . . what a time for the muse to strike!

At least, I thought it had struck. I dropped everything and grabbed a notebook. I was sitting at the table and was about to give birth when the doorbell rang. It rang again, more insistent this time. I tried to put it out of my mind but no! My concentration was shattered. The muse had fled. And so, as I discovered minutes later, had the man with the cap.

Inconvenient, granted, but fired up by the anticipation of greatness, not to mention the business with Rosemary, I stuffed my pockets with copies of Deep Probings, left the stove to its own devices, raced outside and hailed a cab.

'Heathrow,' I cried, elated, 'and there's a hefty tip in it if you break the law.'

I felt sublime. Fame awaited. Cousin Rosemary awaited. I caught my reflection in the rear view mirror and saw that I had metamorphosed, almost without knowing it, into Yeats' 'smiling public man'. The cab driver launched into the obligatory monologue but I wasn't listening. I was undressing cousin Rosemary and basking in the warm glow of a nation's applause. We arrived at our destination with commendable speed and I thrust six copies of my book into the talkative chap's outstretched hand. Six copies at five ninety nine. That's nearly thirty six pounds' worth for a thirty pound fare. Lucky man.

I waved away the change, left the good man to the traffic police and raced inside, but as luck would have it the plane was already gone. The boat. I had to get the boat. I raced back outside and hailed a second cab. A different driver this time, so imagine my surprise then when he launched into a plodding yarn – hilarious to the teller – of a rival's fare being paid in books. I nodded politely but my mind was elsewhere. Rosemary, at this stage, was without hat, gloves and trenchcoat. The applause, deserving to the last ripple, had spread to the European mainland. We arrived at Euston Station with the driver still chortling away. A low fellow, I decided, happy to spend the entire journey mocking his peers. The fare came to twenty nine pounds and eighty pence. Five books. No tip. I raced into the station and was soon on my way to glory.

Rosemary's waistcoat and blouse came off during the course of the train trip and as the boat docked I was removing her boots with a shoe horn while the known world saluted my genius. I had to walk from the boat, since the cover price of Deep Probings was in pounds sterling, not punts. I arrived at the première examining Rosemary's lovely feet for the first time while the entire universe exploded with adulation.

A sizeable crowd of onlookers stood gawping behind metal barriers. I had found the right place anyway. Huge neon letters broadcast the title, The Genius. In smaller letters underneath was the legend: A Man. His Mother. Two Donkeys. Quintessential MacFiach. I tried to force my way through the multitude but, apart from the resistance of the gawpers, I was distracted from my task by the sight of expensive cars disgorging celebrities. Guitar twangers, tub thumpers, strutters and the like.

Also disgorged were members of my immediate circle.

My parents, bent with age.

A slack-jawed Fadharta.

Francis, displaying a nervous twitch and a slightly disconcerting high pitched giggle.

My weeping uncle, his wife and her female lover.

The bland crooner Gilhooley surrounded by a gaggle of simpering spinsters.

McAdoo, Bridie, Doody.

My fourteen other brothers.

A radiant Mr. Scully.

The model for Heaney's publicity shot.

Eventually, by prising my way through the teeming rabble – 'Stand aside!' I bellowed at intervals. 'Make way for MacFiach!' – I managed to reach the barrier. At this moment the preening thespian Fiachra Senior strutted past. He waved foppishly to the gullible masses, who roared their coarse approval. Walking beside him was cousin Rosemary. Fully dressed. Unbearably lovely. Heavy with child.

Heavy with child?! But my passion! My speech! Our scarf-entwined limbs! The typing!! I gripped the metal grille, my knuckles bloodless with rage. Deep in my palpitating breast, primal nature stirred. The beast within. The unbridled monster from the murky depths of my soul. It crawled out of my mouth and let out a roar of righteous ire.

'JEZEBEL!'

I began to climb the barrier. Spurred on by passionate intensity I soon reached the top. A bevy of burly, moustachioed security guards barked obscenities from the other side.

'Do you know who I am!!?' I cried.

They didn't.

deep probings

'I. Am. The Genius.'

They lunged at the barrier, snarling. 'That's me there,' I yelled, pointing at Fiachra Senior. My younger self appeared at just this moment, arm in arm with Widow Bernelle. I pointed at him with delight as I leapt, spring-heeled, from the summit.

'And so,' I whooped triumphantly, 'is that.'